HOUSE OF SHIVERS

GOBLIN MONDAY

R.L. STINE

SCHOLASTIC INC.

Goosebumps book series created by Parachute Press, Inc.
Copyright © 2024 by Scholastic Inc.

ISBN 978-1-338-75225-0

10 9 8 7 6 5 4 3 2 1   24 25 26 27 28

Printed in the U.S.A. 40
First printing 2024

PART
ONE

1

IT ALL STARTED WITH A ROAD TRIP

Am I excited?

How would *you* feel if you were going to see snow for the first time in your life?

My name is Mario Galagos, and I grew up in Key West, Florida. My seventh-grade teacher told us it has never snowed in Key West.

I've never owned a winter coat or gloves until now. I have only two pairs of long pants.

Believe it or not, when I heard I was going to Vermont, I had to look at YouTube videos to see how to build a snowman.

I don't really know Todd and Jewel Simms that well. I moved next door to the Simms family here in Philadelphia only a month ago.

But here I am, making the drive with them to Vermont for school's winter break. I checked online. They've got *mountains* of snow in Vermont.

I'm going to *bury* myself in snow! I've been dreaming about it every night.

Todd is twelve, and Jewel is a year older. When I first met them in their backyard, I thought they were twins. They are exactly the same height, two or three inches shorter than me. They both have springy black hair and dark eyes. And serious faces. Like they're always thinking hard about things.

I don't mean they aren't fun. Jewel has a wicked sense of humor and a great laugh. And Todd is funny, too, in his own quiet way.

We started hanging out together at their house after school. Todd is into a video game called *Crack Me Up.* In the game, you leap off a high mountain cliff. The object of the game is to see how many bones you break when you land. The player who breaks the most bones is the winner.

I thought it was weird at first. But the breaking bones make a great *squish/crack* sound as they shatter, which is kind of fun. My record is four hundred broken bones in two jumps.

Jewel is a big reader. While Todd and I smash our bones, she's usually sitting behind us on the couch with a teen romance on her iPad.

We talk a lot about Florida because they've never been. Todd said it sounds like a strange sun planet in a sci-fi movie where "the sun never sets, and people are trapped in their houses because it's always too hot to go outside."

I tried to explain that's not quite right. But Todd is always making up sci-fi and horror stories. He says he gets it from his grandfather.

More about him later.

Now we are in the Simmses' big SUV, and we are on the highway heading north. Mr. Simms is driving with his wife beside him. Jewel, Todd, and I are in the second row. The third row is piled so high with our stuff, you can't see out the back window.

Of course, Jewel is giving me a hard time about the thing that I brought.

"A leaf blower? Really? Mario, do you really think you're going to find leaves to blow around?"

"It's for the snow," I explained. "I thought maybe I could make snow sculptures with it and—"

"Why do you even *have* a leaf blower?" Todd demanded.

"My dad had a hardware store in Key West," I told them. "He sold a lot of these things. I started playing

3

with leaf blowers when I was four. It was my favorite toy."

They both stared at me. I knew they wanted to make jokes about that, but they were being kind.

"Most people would bring skis," Jewel said finally.

"I've only been on water skis," I said.

Mrs. Simms turned from the front seat. "Mario, this is our favorite family trip," she said. "It's more fun than Christmas. Really."

"That's because of Grandma and Grandpa," Todd said. "You won't *believe* them."

"Tell Mario about your grandparents," Mrs. Simms said.

Jewel chuckled. "I don't know where to begin."

"Describe Grandma Alba to him," their dad said, his eyes straight ahead on the highway.

Jewel thought for a moment. "Uh...well... Grandma Alba is called MomMom, and she's kind of strange and kind of awesome."

"MomMom cooks huge pots of stew," Todd said. "She's always at the stove, stirring her stewpot. And she spends hours knitting strange little outfits that don't fit anyone."

"Tell Mario about her singing," Mrs. Simms said.

Jewel laughed. "MomMom is always bursting into song. She makes everyone sing, too—even though she makes up all the songs. We have to sing along anyway!"

"And she gets mad if we don't get the words right!" Todd added.

A truck rumbled by on the left, shaking the whole SUV. Mr. Simms slowed down a little.

A broad smile crossed Jewel's face. "You haven't heard the best. The best is Grampa Tweety."

"He's a best-selling author," their mom said.

"He is? What does he write?" I asked.

"He writes these fantasy books," Todd said. "Mom, what are the titles?"

"They are hugely popular all over the world," Mrs. Simms said. "Two of his most famous ones are *The Big Book of Imps & Trolls* and *Fairies, Sprites, & Elves I Have Known.*"

"His name is Harlan, but everyone calls him Grampa Tweety," Jewel said. "That's because he is a fanatic bird-watcher. He can do hundreds of birdcalls. You name the bird, he can do it."

"Wow," I muttered. "Amazing."

"And he keeps a huge, floor-to-ceiling birdcage in his living room," Todd added. "It's jam-packed with chirping birds. They chirp day and night."

"Whoa!" I exclaimed. "A giant floor-to-ceiling bird-cage in the living room! I can't even picture it! That's awesome!"

Of course, when I said that, I had no idea I would soon end up trapped inside that birdcage—fighting for my life.

A HAPPY START

"Mario, I can't believe you brought a leaf blower," Mr. Simms said. He pulled it out of the back of the SUV and handed it to me.

"I have some fun ideas for it," I said. "You'll see."

My first steps in the snow were awesome. There was at least a foot on the ground, and taller snowdrifts had piled up around the backyard. Most of the snow in the driveway had been shoveled, but there was a thin layer left that crunched under my boots.

I bent down and scooped up a handful of snow from the yard. It was still powdery. Cold and wet. I squeezed it into the shape of a snowball.

Can you imagine?

My first snowball?

The afternoon sun made the snow gleam like silver. So bright it was almost blinding.

I felt like a five-year-old. I wanted to run around and

fall to the ground and make snow angels and roll in it and bury myself in the drifts.

We were unpacking the SUV. Grandma Alba and Grampa Tweety watched from their kitchen door. I couldn't wait to unload my camera. I needed to start taking snow photos.

Yes, I brought a camera with a lot of different lenses. Taking photos with your phone is for amateurs.

Mr. Simms handed me my camera case. "I'm going to do a photo essay for my winter break project," I said.

"That's great," he replied. "Our family never remembers to take pictures. Don't forget to send them to us!"

I gazed around. A big garden shed stood at the back of the yard. One side of the garden was edged with shrubs and tall weeds. The other side was enclosed by a wall. A wide garden area stretched in between.

All the plants and shrubs were draped in snow. Nothing was blooming since it was the middle of winter. I still wasn't used to that. In Florida, plants and trees bloom all year.

Mr. Simms lugged two more bags from the car. He had a big smile on his face. "This is going to be the best winter break ever!" he said.

I started to reply when something hard hit the back of my coat. I let out a cry and stumbled forward.

"Gotcha!" Todd yelled.

I spun around. Todd scooped up another snowball.

"Snowball fight!" I cried. I began to set down the leaf blower and camera case. "Can we have a snowball fight?"

"Later," Mr. Simms said. "Let's go talk with Grandma and Grampa. It's almost dinnertime."

We stepped into the kitchen, and there were lots of hugs. Lots of happy greetings. I think Todd and Jewel were as excited to be here as I was.

A big pot of stew simmered on the stove. I heard birds chirping loudly in the front room.

Grandma Alba and Grampa Tweety reminded me of elves I'd seen in a graphic novel. I mean, they were both shorter than me and kind of round. And they both had turned-up noses and even their ears looked a little pointy. Seriously.

Grampa had wide, red suspenders holding up his baggy pants. He wore a faded lumberjack shirt with some of the buttons missing.

He was completely bald except for a thin clump of

white hair at the top of his head that stood straight up. His blue eyes sparkled like jewels. And he kept bouncing up and down, repeating, "A great day upon us. A great day upon us . . ."

Grandma had shiny white hair pulled back in a bun. Her dark eyes squinted at us behind thick, square eyeglasses. She wore a purple dress with a white apron over it that read: *Kiss the Cook*. She never stopped grinning.

She pinched Todd's cheeks and then moved on to Jewel's cheeks. *Pinch. Pinch.* She had the tiniest hands I ever saw on a person. Doll's hands.

"That stew smells awesome, Grandma Alba," I said.

"Call me MomMom, Mario. Everyone else does."

I took a step back. I think she wanted to pinch my cheeks, too!

Jewel grabbed my hand and pulled me into the living room. "Come on, Mario. You have to see the birdcage."

"Whoa!" I let out a cry when I saw it. The wire cage rose to the ceiling and took up nearly half the room. Birds chattered and squawked. They flew up and down and dropped from perch to perch.

How many? Maybe two dozen birds. All colors and sizes. I recognized some tiny white finches because my cousin had finches down in Florida. Two bright red birds sat together on a high perch. And on a lower perch, two adorable blue-gray birds with yellow wing tips leaned against each other, cooing softly.

"What are those birds?" I asked. "They are the cutest."

"Lovebirds," Jewel said. "Don't they look like they're really in love?"

"Do you believe this bird collection?" Todd said. "Grampa Tweety is amazing."

"Does he photograph them?" I asked. "Or write about them?"

Jewel shook her head. "I think he just likes to look at them."

"It's a good show," I said. "I want to take some photos."

"Tweety is a collector," Jewel said. "He collects weird stories, and he collects birds."

"Dinnertime! Come to the table," Mrs. Simms called from the next room.

A few minutes later, we were seated around a long table that ran next to one kitchen wall. Silver serving dishes gleamed on the white tablecloth. The room was very warm, and the tangy food aromas made my stomach growl.

MomMom stood at the stove, stirring the stew.

Glass doors looked out onto the garden, where it was gently snowing. The flakes started to coat the bare tree limbs. The lawn furniture was covered with canvas bags, and a layer of snow gathered on them, too.

I couldn't contain my excitement. "Real winter!" I cried. "I can't believe I'm in real winter!"

This is going to be the best vacation of my life! I told myself. *The best!*

Are you wondering when things started to turn bad? Just wait.

FIREFLY FREAKS OUT

MomMom served the stew in big clay bowls. Tweety passed around puffy dinner rolls for dunking. The food was delicious.

Tweety sat at the head of the long table. In between spoonfuls of stew, he would tweet at the birds in the other room. Each time, a bird would answer him. That always made him grin.

He slurped his stew noisily. Gravy dripped onto his chin, but he didn't seem to notice. His bright blue eyes twinkled happily.

I watched the snow falling in the garden. *First thing tomorrow morning, I'll take my camera and go on a walk,* I decided.

"What are you working on, Grampa Tweety?" Jewel asked.

He finally picked up his napkin and wiped the gravy from his chin.

"I'm writing a story about a Pukwudgie," he told her. "Fascinating fellow. You probably never heard of a Pukwudgie."

We all shook our heads. "Never," Todd muttered.

"He's a figure from Native American legends," Tweety explained. "He looks like a small human from the front. But he has quills like a porcupine down his back." Tweety chuckled. "Very ornery critters. They can shape-shift, and they love to play mean tricks on humans."

"Do you think they're real?" I asked. "I'd like to take some photos of a Pukwudgie for my photo essay."

Tweety laughed: "You probably won't run into any *this* week, Mario."

Jewel raised her hand toward Tweety. "Grampa, please pass the rolls. MomMom, this is the best stew you ever made."

MomMom's round face turned red. "Don't flatter an old woman."

"She's right," Todd said. "I mean, I could eat that whole pot."

MomMom suddenly pushed her chair back and climbed to her feet. "Let's all put our spoons down," she said. "Let's sing my favorite winter song. Actually, it's a Christmas song."

Todd leaned close and whispered in my ear. "Uh-oh. Here we go. Just do your best. Move your lips and pretend to sing."

MomMom raised her spoon like a conductor's baton. "Everybody sing along," she said.

She cleared her throat loudly and began to sing:

The old man is coming,
There's barley in the barn.
The old man will watch you
When you wake up Christmas morn.
The old man will give you a plum.
Give you a plum. He'll give you a plum.
Don't bite it, don't taste it, not on Christmas morn.

She started a second verse, waving her spoon baton. But she stopped after a few words.

Her face turned red again. "Why isn't anyone singing?" she demanded.

"We don't know that song, MomMom," Todd answered.

"*Everyone* knows that song!" she exclaimed.

Something rubbed against my legs. I looked down and saw Firefly, their black cat, staring up at me.

MomMom made a grumpy sound and dropped back on her chair.

Jewel patted her hand. "It's an awesome song, MomMom," she told her. "Will you teach it to me later?"

"You already know it, Jewel. Everyone knows the 'Barley in the Barn' song. We sang it in kindergarten."

Grampa Tweety rolled his eyes. "Let's eat and do our singing after dinner."

"MomMom, you've never given me the recipe for this stew," Mrs. Simms said. I knew she was trying to change the subject. "You really must share it with me."

MomMom shook her head. "I can't. It's a *secret* recipe."

Something caught my eye in the garden. Peering through the glass door, I saw two tall brown rabbits. They were standing side by side on their hind legs, looking in at us.

I jumped up. "I have to take a picture," I said. I ran to my room to get my camera.

When I returned, the rabbits were still standing there. I stepped to the glass doors and started to snap some shots.

But something bumped my legs and nearly knocked me over.

Firefly the cat. The creature let out a long, loud *hiss*.

He raised onto his hind legs and attacked the door. Pounded the glass with both front paws. Shrieking and clawing and scratching, the cat went berserk.

I turned to Grampa Tweety. "Wh-wh-what's wrong with Firefly?" I stammered.

Tweety shrugged. "It's probably the goblin in the garden."

4

BE PREPARED

Firefly shrieked and threw himself against the glass.

MomMom picked him up and stroked his back. His black fur stood straight up. It took her a long time to calm him.

The cat's cries had disturbed the birds. In the other room, they were squawking and screeching.

The two rabbits had run away. I set down my camera and took my seat at the kitchen table.

I turned to Tweety. "Did you say something about a goblin?" I asked him.

"If you don't bother him, he won't bother you," Tweety replied.

I stared at him. Was he making some kind of joke? What kind of answer was that?

"A goblin?" I said. "Really? You're not making that up?"

He dipped a roll into his stew bowl. "My stories are all true," he said.

"I've seen goblins in video games," I said. "But . . . I never thought they were real."

"Lots of things are real," Tweety replied.

Was he just being mysterious?

"Then I'd love to take some photos of a goblin," I said.

Tweety shook his head. "You don't want to do that, Mario. They can be mean—and they don't like having their pictures taken."

That made everyone at the table laugh.

I finally caught on. "I get it," I said. "This is the Simmses' family joke. Scare the new kid. Okay, okay. I'm catching on."

Tweety bit off half of his roll and swallowed it. "I'm not trying to scare you, Mario. I just want you to be prepared."

Prepared for a goblin?

I laughed. He wouldn't let the joke drop.

MomMom jumped to her feet and started clearing the stew bowls from the table. "Can we stop talking about goblins?" she said. "I'm about to serve my famous plumpkin pie."

"Plumpkin pie?" I said.

Jewel laughed. "That's because it's impossible not to get plump when you eat it."

19

Their grandparents are so cute and fun, I thought.

I loved that the family shared so many jokes.

MomMom's dessert was the best pumpkin pie I'd ever had. Luckily, she had made an enormous one. Because everyone wanted a second slice.

When we were finished, Tweety led us into the living room. In the big cage, the birds had quieted down. Most of them were hunched on their perches. The lovebirds cooed softly together.

"I have a present for everyone," Tweety announced.

He disappeared for a few minutes. Then he returned with a bunch of pendants dangling from his neck. He slipped one off and held it up.

"I have pendants for everyone," he said. "And I don't want you to go anywhere without them."

He handed the first one to Todd. It was a green ribbon with some kind of metal pouch on it.

"You really want us to wear these?" I asked.

He handed me one and waited until I lowered it around my neck.

"What is inside it?" I asked.

"Nutmeg," Tweety answered. "Goblins stay away from nutmeg. The aroma makes them weak and puts them to sleep."

"Tweety, stop," MomMom said. "You're scaring everyone."

But he didn't stop. "You need these for protection," he said. "The goblins get hungry in the winter when the garden is bare."

AN IMP IN THE LAUNDRY ROOM

Was he serious?

His blue eyes twinkled when he spoke. I decided he was making up a story. I think he enjoys scaring people.

"Tweety, I'm begging you," MomMom said. "Please stop. Let's talk about something else." Her eyes flashed. "Should we sing another song?"

"It's okay, Alma. I just want them to be prepared," he replied. He handed pendants to Mr. and Mrs. Simms.

I stepped close to Jewel and whispered in her ear. "He's kidding, right? It's a joke?"

She whispered back. "Of course he's kidding. But they're both so *adorable*, aren't they?"

"Tell us a story, Dad," Mr. Simms said. "I've been looking forward to hearing your stories."

Tweety snapped his suspenders. "A true story," he said. "My stories are all true. Sit down, everyone. I'll tell you what happened to me just last week."

We all sat in a circle in the living room. Todd and Jewel's parents sat on the frayed red velvet couch. The rest of us sat in worn brown leather chairs. The only sounds were the crackle of a low fire in the fireplace and the flutter of birds' wings in the tall cage.

Tweety raised a white coffee mug and took a long drink. Then he settled back into his chair. I noticed that his feet didn't reach the floor. I started to chuckle but stopped myself.

"Last week, I found an imp in the laundry room," he said. He paused to see our reaction.

No one said anything. We waited for him to continue.

"As you can imagine," he said, spinning the coffee mug in his hands, "I was surprised. Imps aren't like elves. They are very rare. And they are very good at not getting caught."

He took another long drink.

I had to ask: "What exactly is an imp?"

"Good question, Mario," he replied. "Imps are nasty little creatures. They're not cute. They have claws and sharp teeth. Some of them are bearded. Some have horns. Their skin can have bright colors. But believe me, they're not nice to look at."

He set his coffee mug down. "A lot of people think

23

imps are just characters in myths. That they don't exist," he continued. "But I know they are real. Especially since I trapped one last week."

Birds suddenly squawked in the cage behind us.

"Imps are not evil," Tweety said. "They don't kill unless threatened. They like to play tricks on humans. But they mostly stay hidden."

"Did you write about imps in your books?" I asked.

He nodded. "Yes. But I'd never met one until last week."

I studied Tweety as he talked. Of course, he was making up the story. But his face was so serious. He never cracked a smile. And his eyes stared steadily at the fire.

It was hard not to believe him.

Todd sat closest to Tweety. He had his legs tucked under him in the big armchair. "How did the imp get into the laundry room?" Todd asked.

Tweety scratched his nose. "I have no idea. It was last Thursday morning. MomMom and I were getting the house ready for your visit."

"We had to clean the guest rooms," MomMom said.

"I carried a big armful of bedsheets to the laundry

room," Tweety said. "And when I stepped inside, I saw something strange."

"What did you see?" Todd asked.

"The washing machine lid was open. And there was a little creature in it. Splashing away. Taking a bath."

"Whoa!" The Simmses all burst out in surprise.

I stared at them. Did they really believe this story? Or were they just pretending to believe it to make Tweety happy?

"I dropped the bedsheets," Tweety continued. "I stumbled toward the washer. I recognized what kind of creature he was immediately. He had a sharp beard and long, pointy ears. An imp. An actual imp."

"Dad, what did you do?" Mr. Simms asked.

"I couldn't do anything. As soon as the imp saw me, he started splashing waves of hot water on me. I had to duck away."

Tweety shook his head. "The imp leaped out of the washer. He ran to his clothes. They were piled up on the floor in the corner. He pulled them on, and then he turned to run out of the laundry room."

"Didn't you try to stop him?" Todd asked.

"Of *course*," Tweety answered. "I wanted to keep

him there. I wanted to try to talk with him. So I tried to block his path."

"But he got away?" Todd asked.

Tweety nodded. "The imp leaped high into the air. He ran on top of my head with his bare feet. His toe-nails scratched my forehead. Then he disappeared out the door."

We all kept our gaze on Grampa Tweety. No one spoke for a long moment.

He's such a good storyteller, I told myself. *He could make you believe anything. Even a story as crazy as this one.*

Tweety glanced around the room. "You don't believe me?" he said. "You think I'm making up a story?"

"It—it's a good story," I said.

Tweety jumped down off the chair. "Follow me," he said. "I'll show you something." He waved with both hands. "Come on. You can decide if it's a story or not."

His boots clomped on the wooden floor as he led us all down a back hall. He stopped at the end and pushed open a door. "The laundry room," he said.

He stepped in and clicked on a ceiling light. A pale glow washed over the room.

We squeezed inside. There was only room for a washer and a dryer.

26

Tweety pointed to the floor. "Down there. In the corner. The imp escaped in a hurry. He left his jacket."

We all turned. I squinted hard.

"Oh, wow," I said.

A tiny brown leather jacket lay crumpled in the corner of the room.

DEAD IN THE GARDEN

"Tweety's stories are so awesome," Todd said. "That's how I got into fantasy stories and sci-fi. I hope I got some storytelling skills from him."

"But . . . the imp thing . . ." I said. "That was just a story, right? It's hard to tell with your grampa. Sometimes it looks like he actually believes the story."

Todd laughed. "I know. Sometimes, Jewel and I don't know *what* to believe. I guess that's what makes him such a good storyteller."

He pulled his pajama shirt over his head. Then he climbed up to the top bunk.

He and I were sharing a bunk bed in an upstairs guest room. I gazed out the window. Down below, the snow glowed silver under a full moon. It seemed to stretch on forever. Wind rustled the bare plants and shrubs in the garden and sent sheets of snow flying in the air.

I couldn't stop thinking about the imp story. It

couldn't be real. But Tweety seemed so serious about it. Wouldn't he crack a smile if he was making it up to scare us?

I couldn't stop picturing the tiny leather jacket on the laundry room floor.

"Hey, Todd." I slipped under the covers of the bottom bunk. "Didn't Jewel say something about MomMom knitting little outfits when we were in the car?"

I heard Todd turn over onto his side. His head poked down from the top bunk. "Yeah. She's a good knitter. But her stuff never fits anyone." He chuckled. "Once, she knitted a sweater with three sleeves."

"So, do you think she made that little imp jacket?" I said.

He shook his upside-down head. "No way, Mario. The jacket was leather. She only knits. She doesn't do leather."

"So where do you think that little jacket came from?" I asked.

He disappeared back up to his bunk. "Well—"

He didn't get to answer.

We both heard a squeal. Followed by a shrill scream. And a high wail of pain that lasted a few seconds and then cut off sharply.

I heard heavy thuds in the snow. Someone running?

I leaped out of the bunk, listening for more sounds or another scream. I darted to the window. Todd dropped down to the floor and came up behind me.

We both stared down at the garden.

"Oh, wow," I murmured. "Oh no."

I stared at the rabbit sprawled on its side. Not moving. Not moving. Dead.

I squinted hard and gasped. Its belly had been ripped out.

Dark blood puddled around the corpse on the silvery snow.

CAGED

I couldn't get to sleep.

Every time I closed my eyes, I saw that dead rabbit in the snow. Its guts pulled out. Lying there on its side in a dark puddle of blood.

What wild animal would kill it like that and then leave it there? Not eat it? Not drag it away for later?

Todd thought maybe it was a wolf. Or a coyote.

But the rabbit hadn't been eaten. Just pulled apart.

We went back to the bunk bed. I shut my eyes tight and started to count down from one hundred. Sometimes that helped me drift off to sleep.

Not tonight.

I turned onto one side, then the other.

"Hey, Todd," I whispered up to the top bunk. "Are you awake?"

Silence.

"Are you up?"

I heard a muttered, hoarse reply that didn't make any sense. He was asleep.

I turned and lowered my feet to the floor. I stood up and crossed to the window.

I peered down to the backyard. But the moon had floated behind some clouds, and it was too dark to see the rabbit corpse.

I shuddered.

My mouth suddenly felt as dry as cotton. I decided to get a glass of water.

The wood floor was cold, but I didn't want to bother with shoes or socks.

I stepped into the hall. A dim gray light washed up from downstairs. I grabbed the banister and made my way down.

I headed to the kitchen but stopped when I saw that the light was coming from the living room. I heard the soft fluttering of wings and a low warbling, "*Coo, coo, coo.*"

My bare feet moved silently over the floor. I stopped at the wide doorway to the living room. I squinted into the gray light until the big birdcage came into focus.

It took me a while to realize what I was seeing. I clapped a hand over my mouth to keep from making a sound.

And stared at Grampa Tweety . . . Grampa Tweety standing *inside the cage.*

He walked slowly back and forth, shuffling his feet over the cage floor. And in his hands . . . he had a lovebird cupped in each palm. He held the birds close to his face and cooed at them. Then he rubbed them on his cheeks.

Rubbed them on his cheeks . . . and walked slowly back and forth . . . back and forth . . .

WILL THINGS GET STRANGER?

Saturday morning, we all took our places at the long table for breakfast. Outside the glass doors, the wind had stopped gusting. The snow had settled. Everything in the garden stood still as a photograph.

Staring into the bright glare of sunlight, I looked for the dead rabbit, but I couldn't find it. All that remained was a small pink stain on the snow.

Grampa Tweety dropped into his place at the end of the table. "We'll go bird-watching this morning, Mario," he said. "Give you a bigger taste of your first snow."

"I can't wait," I replied.

I stared at him, thinking hard. *Should I tell him I saw him last night inside the cage?*

Should I just forget about it?

"Grampa Tweety, I saw you last night," I blurted. That's what happens when I'm nervous. The words just tumble out of my mouth.

Grampa was wiping his fork and knife with his napkin. He looked up at me. "Saw me?"

"I—I couldn't sleep," I said. "I came downstairs for a glass of water. And . . . I saw you in the birdcage."

He swept a hand back over his bald head. "Mario, I go into the cage a lot," he said. "I do have to clean it, you know."

"Well, sure," I said. "But—"

"And I like to be close to my birds," he added. "They're very special to me."

Close to his birds? Rubbing them on his face?

Todd and Jewel were staring at me. I couldn't figure out what they were thinking.

"If you're going out in the cold, you'd better have a hearty breakfast," MomMom said. She carried a big skillet of eggs and ham slices to the table. She used a long spatula to place the food on our plates. Then she stood behind her seat, wiping her tiny hands on her apron.

"Before we eat, let's sing the 'Saturday Morning Breakfast' song," she said. "I know you all know it, so join in."

She banged a rhythm on the tabletop with a spoon and began to sing:

Which came first?
The eggs or the ham?
Which came first
to fry in the pan?
The old man is watching as breakfast is nigh.
We eat our ham and we don't ask why.
Don't ask why. Don't ask why.
We eat our ham and send our praise to the sky.
Which came first?
The eggs or the ham?
Which—

She stopped suddenly, and her face turned red. "Why am I the only one singing?" she demanded. "Come on, everyone. You know we always sing the breakfast song on Saturday."

"They don't know that song," Tweety said from the other end of the table. He had already started on his eggs. "Because you just made it up."

MomMom frowned at him. "They could still sing along."

"Sit down," Tweety said, motioning with one hand. "You don't want our guest to think we're strange, do you?"

I laughed. They were definitely strange. And everybody at the table *loved* that they were strange.

Would things soon start to get stranger?

Three guesses.

"I THINK WE'RE BEING FOLLOWED!"

After breakfast, we bundled into our parkas, wool hats, boots, and gloves. I strapped my camera case over my shoulder. Then we followed Grampa Tweety out the back door and into the snow.

"Where are Mom and Dad?" Jewel asked.

Tweety rolled his eyes. "They are wimps. They decided to stay indoors and keep warm. They said they wanted to keep MomMom company."

I took a few steps from the house. My boots crunched noisily over the snow. The cold made my face tingle!

A light snow was falling. I felt as if I was walking in a snow globe.

I slipped my camera case off my shoulder and set it down. Then I pulled off my gloves and jammed them into my parka pockets. I dug both hands into the snow and picked up a big chunk. I squeezed the snow into a snowball.

I tossed it at a tall pine tree. But I didn't throw it hard enough, and it sank into the snow.

I rubbed my hands in the snow. I pressed a powdery chunk against my face. I wanted to lie down and roll around in it. But the others were watching me.

Jewel and Todd both laughed. "We get it," Jewel said. "Your first snow."

"You don't know how long I've dreamed about this," I said. "It's like . . . It's like . . ."

I couldn't think what it was like.

Grampa Tweety slapped his gloves together. "Let's get to the trees," he said. "This is the best hour to see birds."

My hands were red and frozen. I pulled my gloves back on, strapped on my camera case, and followed them across the lawn.

Behind the garden was the start of a small forest. The trees were bare. Snow clung to their branches.

I narrowed my eyes to a squint as we walked. The sun glare off the snow was so bright, it made my eyes water.

Grampa Tweety stopped a few feet from the nearest tree. He cupped his hands around his mouth and sent up a bird tweet. "*Tweeet, tweet-tweet.*" He repeated it a few times.

And then the same tweet rang down from a high branch in a tree.

Tweety did his birdcall again. And again, the bird in the tree replied with the same tweet.

Tweety pointed to the branch. I saw a small grayish-tan bird perched up there.

"It's a common house finch," he said. "But doesn't he have a lovely call?"

He called up to the bird again. I pulled out my camera and snapped several shots.

We moved through the trees. Tweety stopped and let out a different call.

A small bluebird fluttered into view and came to a landing on a low branch. I pushed past Todd and Jewel and started taking its picture. Luckily, I'd remembered my zoom lens.

Tweety pointed to three big black birds perched in the next tree. "Those crows are always here," he said. "I don't know why these birds didn't go south for the winter." He chuckled. "Too lazy, maybe."

I stepped under the branch and snapped photos of the crows.

Jewel tugged off her gloves and pulled a bag from her coat pocket. "I brought birdseed," she said. She poured a pile of the little brown seeds into her hand.

"Give me some," Todd said, shoving his hand at her.

She poured seeds into his hand. Then the two of them stood perfectly still with their palms raised high.

Grampa Tweety pressed his lips in a long birdcall.

A few seconds later, a bird with a red head and a pale red belly fluttered down to us and came to a rest on Jewel's wrist. The bird lowered its head and pecked at the seeds. Jewel kept her hand steady and didn't move.

I snapped a few photos.

"It's a red-bellied woodpecker," Tweety said. "They live here year-round."

He waved his gloved hand. "Let's keep moving. Lots more to see, but we don't want to be in the cold much longer." He tightened his scarf around his neck and began to crunch over the snow.

Todd and Jewel followed. I fell behind because I had trouble putting the camera back into its case. My hands were frozen even inside my gloves, and I had to try three times to snap the case closed.

I began to trot to catch up with them. But I stopped when I heard a sound behind me.

A crunch of snow.

Was someone there?

I spun around and saw a dark shadow slide across the snow. It vanished behind a tall shrub.

I stopped and squinted hard. Nothing moved.

After a few seconds, I turned and started walking toward the others.

Again, I heard a *crunch* behind me.

This time, I didn't turn around. I kept walking. Listening.

Another soft *crunch*. Yes. Definitely. Footsteps behind me.

You know that tingling at the back of your neck when you have a feeling someone is watching you?

My neck was definitely tingling. I could feel someone's eyes on my back.

I twisted around quickly to try to catch sight of them. Again, a shadow darted out of view.

A chill ran down my back.

"Hey," I called. "Is someone there?"

I knew someone was there. Who was it? Why didn't they show themselves?

I leaned forward and started to run. "Grampa Tweety!" I called. "Hey, wait! I think we're being followed!"

IS IT A GOBLIN?

Tweety, Todd, and Jewel were gazing up at a tiny orange bird on a low tree branch. I ran up to them, struggling to catch my breath.

"Back there," I choked out. "By those shrubs." I pointed. "Someone following us."

They all turned and looked past me.

"Is it a goblin?" Tweety said.

"Huh?" Another chill gripped the back of my neck. "Are you serious?"

He laughed.

Todd gave me a shove. "You're starting to believe Grampa Tweety's stories?"

"I—I—I—" I stammered. I pointed again. "There's someone there. I heard them. I saw their shadow—"

"It's the sun reflecting off the bright snow," Jewel said. She pulled off her sunglasses. "Here, Mario. Do you want to borrow these?"

I shook my head. "No thanks."

We all stared across the snow. A strong burst of wind sent a sheet of powder into the air. If the person had left footsteps in the snow, the gust had blown them away.

"No worries," Tweety said. He turned back to the tree. "Mario, did you see the goldfinch?"

"No. I—"

"The goldfinch is very shy. It takes all my bird-calling skill to get him to show himself."

"How did you learn so many birdcalls?" I asked him.

A smile crossed his face. "I've been walking here and watching the birds for a hundred fifty years," he said. "I just picked up a few birdcalls at a time."

Todd laughed. "Grampa, you don't look a day over a hundred forty!" he said.

We all laughed.

"We'd better head back to the house," Tweety said. He squeezed his nose. "My face feels like a big ice cube."

We turned and started to walk back. I kept my eyes on the line of shrubs at the side of the yard. Was someone crouching back there, watching us from behind them? I didn't see anyone.

Maybe I *had* imagined it.

Suddenly, I stopped. I couldn't resist. Being in this

awesome snow was too exciting for me. I set down my camera case and let out a "Whooop!"

Then I tossed myself to the ground and rolled around like a maniac in the snow. I saw the others watching me. But I didn't care. I had no choice. I had to do it.

Snow oozed under my coat collar and down my back. I stood up and brushed the powdery white stuff from my hair with both hands. Then I shook myself hard, sending snow spraying from my coat and pants.

"You're happy now?" Jewel asked.

I nodded. "Happy."

We started to walk again. The house came into view.

We followed Tweety through the garden. Patches of snow covered the canvas bags draped over the lawn furniture. The garden was sad, everything bare and wilted.

The three of them walked ahead of me. They were nearly to the glass doors when I saw it.

I gasped. Stopped. Stared.

At first, I thought it was a boy. He was about my size. But he didn't have a boy's face. He had an animal face, green fur, pointy ears.

He stood half-hidden by the tall, dry stalks at the edge of the yard. Were those horns poking up from the top of his head?

He stared hard at me with catlike eyes, black and glowing.

"Noooo!" A cry escaped my throat. A goblin!

I tried to fight back my fear. But my whole body shuddered. The camera case slipped off my shoulder and thudded onto the snow.

I called to the others, "Hey—look! Look! Help me!"

But they were already in the house. The glass doors closed behind them.

"Hey, goblin!" I called.

The creature moved quickly. Snarling like an angry animal, he lowered himself and came scrabbling toward me on all fours.

I tried to back away, but my boots slipped in the snow.

I turned to run inside—and the creature leaped onto my back.

"No! Nooooo! Off! Get *off*!" I screamed.

He gripped my shoulders and wrapped his legs around my middle. I felt his hot breath on the back of my neck.

I spun quickly. Gave a hard toss. Twisted my whole body. And sent the snarling creature flying off me.

With a frightened cry, I grabbed my camera bag and swung it at him.

The leather bag hit him in the chest. He staggered back on his hind legs.

The blow seemed to stun him. He stood there, breathing hard, staring at me with those dark cat eyes.

My whole body was shaking. I had to get a photo of him. I fumbled with the camera case and managed to open it. I let the case fall to the snow and raised the camera to my eye.

"Yes!" I snapped a photo of the creature.

The sound of the camera seemed to startle him. With a final growl, he turned and galloped away, his paws kicking up waves of snow as he ran.

I stumbled into the kitchen, struggling to catch my breath.

Jewel turned away from the fridge. "Mario, what's wrong? What took you so long?"

"A g-goblin," I stammered. "It grabbed me and—"

Todd set down the glass of water he'd been drinking. He hurried over to me. "A *what*?" he demanded. "What grabbed you?"

"A goblin," I said, still breathless. "Where is Grampa Tweety? I have to tell him—"

Jewel laughed. "Good one, Mario. Very funny."

"You're such a good actor. You almost fooled *me*," Todd said.

"No. No. It . . . climbed on my back. It *attacked* me!" I cried.

They both laughed.

"Stop laughing!" I screamed. "It isn't a joke." Then I remembered the photo. "I . . . I have proof. It's real. Look. I'll show you."

My hands were shaking so hard, it took three tries to press the button on the camera. Finally, it turned on, and I slid my thumb over the screen until I found the last photo.

"Here. Look," I said. I raised the screen to their faces.

Jewel and Todd both gasped.

11

TWEETY ISN'T SURPRISED

"Nice photo of snow," Jewel said.

"Huh? What are you talking about?" I cried. I spun the camera around and gazed at the screen.

I saw the snowy ground in front of the garden. The tall, dry stalks at the side.

But no creature. No goblin standing there on two legs staring at me.

"But—but—" I sputtered.

"Was the goblin invisible?" Todd asked. He and his sister laughed.

A long sigh escaped my mouth. I stared at the screen. I didn't know what to say.

"Attack of the Invisible Goblin!" Todd said in a deep movie announcer voice. "I've been trying to think of an idea for my next story. Thanks, Mario!" He slapped me on the back.

"Okay, okay," I muttered. "I was shaking. My hands

were shaking. I must have just missed him. He must have moved by the time I pressed the shutter."

I tucked the camera back into its case. *No way* they were going to believe me. I wanted to get away from them so I could think.

I went up to my room and pulled off my parka and boots. I set the camera case on the desk. I dropped onto the edge of the lower bunk.

But I didn't have time to think. Jewel and Todd stepped into the room grinning. "Grampa Tweety tells some great stories!" Todd said.

"Don't you think it's possible that they're real?" I replied. "He told us his stories are all true. And he's very convincing."

"I write scary stories, too," Todd said. "You read some of them. But you didn't believe them—did you?"

"That's different," I muttered. "This creature . . . it—it attacked me, and—"

"I know what the monster was in the garden," Jewel said.

"What was it?" I demanded.

"A raccoon," she said.

"No way!" I cried. "It—"

"I've seen really big raccoons up here," Jewel said.

50

"It walked on two legs," I said. "It had green fur and horns on its head. It leaped onto my back."

"Why wasn't it in your photo?" Todd demanded.

"I told you. I was terrified. I was shaking," I said. "I must have bumped the camera."

"Raccoons have been known to attack," Jewel said.

"Stop," I said. "Just stop. I know what I saw, and it wasn't a raccoon."

I turned to Todd. "Grampa Tweety writes books about elves and fairies and imps, right? Does he believe any of them are real?"

"Hard to tell," Todd answered.

He started to say more. But MomMom shouted from downstairs. "Lunchtime! Come down, everyone! Lunchtime!"

In the kitchen, Grampa Tweety snapped his suspenders and stretched his arms above his head. "That was a good hike this morning," he said. His nose was still red from the cold.

He dropped into his chair at the end of the long table. He picked up his soup spoon and wiped it clean with his napkin.

I sat down and gazed out the glass doors. Was that creature still in the garden? No. No sign of him.

I looked for footprints. But it had started to snow again, and it was coming down hard now. I couldn't see any.

I wanted to tell Grampa Tweety about him. But I had no proof. Tweety would probably laugh at me, too.

MomMom stood at the other end of the table, ladling a thick, green soup from her big pot into soup bowls. "Hope you like Forest Peapod Soup," she said. "It's my own special recipe. And I picked the peas myself."

She placed a bowl in front of me, and I took a long sniff. "Smells great," I said. Actually, it smelled kind of funky. Like grass and dirt. I hoped it tasted better than it smelled.

I blew on the spoon. The soup was steaming hot. I tried half a spoonful. Not bad. Kind of sweet, actually.

"Grampa Tweety, Mario saw something in the garden," Todd said.

Tweety slurped a big spoonful of soup. "I'm not surprised," he said.

I set my spoon down. "What was it?" I demanded. "The creature . . . it attacked me. Was it a goblin? He was short with green fur and had these cat eyes—"

Tweety opened his mouth to answer.

But a deafening *screech* made us all gasp.

I felt something brush past my legs. Another loud *screech*.

The cat. Firefly. He tore past us to the doors and leaped onto them with his whole body, as if trying to smash his way through the glass.

Hissing and screeching, the big black cat scratched the doors frantically, pawing and punching.

I jumped to my feet. "Did Firefly see it? Did he see the creature?" I cried.

"WHERE ARE MOM AND DAD?"

Firefly let out a long, final *hiss*. Then he sank to all fours and stood gazing into the garden, his chest heaving, his breath rapid and noisy.

I ran to the door. I pressed my face against the glass and peered out.

The snow was coming down in sheets now. I squinted hard, but I couldn't see a thing.

"I don't know what Firefly saw," Tweety said. "Could have been a rabbit. Probably a rabbit."

Whoa. Once again, I pictured that rabbit from last night, dead in the snow with its stomach ripped out.

I shook that picture from my mind, returned to the table, and slid back into my chair.

"Firefly is so nervous. That's why we named him Firefly," Tweety said. "Because he darts back and forth like a firefly caught in a jar."

"Do you believe in goblins?" I didn't really mean to ask the question. But I told you, that's what happens when I'm upset. I just blurt things out.

Tweety dropped his soup spoon. "Believe in goblins?" he repeated.

He and MomMom burst out laughing.

"That's like asking, 'Do you believe in trees?'" Tweety said.

"But most people *don't* believe in them!" I exclaimed.

Grampa Tweety shook his head. "Most people don't know *what* they believe. Alma and I try to keep an open mind."

"Hey, wait a minute!" Jewel suddenly cried. She had been quiet the whole lunch. But now she gazed around the room, her face twisted in confusion. "Where are Mom and Dad?"

Todd blinked. "Yeah. Where are they? We were so hung up about the creature in the garden . . ."

We all turned to MomMom.

She shrugged. "I don't know. I don't know where they went."

"But . . . this morning you said they were going to stay home and keep you company," Todd said.

MomMom nodded. "Yes. We had a short talk. But then they disappeared." She thought for a moment. "Oh. I remember. They said they wanted to take a walk."

Jewel squinted at her. "They went for a walk and didn't come home in time for lunch? And the storm is getting bad out there now."

"I'm sure we'll see them very soon," Tweety chimed in. "They're used to this kind of weather. Maybe they'll have some stories to tell. Maybe they saw a goblin in the garden." He hee-hawed as if he'd made a funny joke.

"Finish your soup. It's getting cold," MomMom said.

We all picked up our spoons again. But Todd and Jewel kept glancing at each other. They kept turning to the empty seats where their parents should have been sitting.

Todd pulled out his phone. He studied the screen. "Weird," he muttered. "They always send us a text when they are going out."

He swiped the screen and punched in a number. "I'll call Dad. See where they are."

He frowned and lowered the phone. "It went right to voice mail."

"You shouldn't worry," MomMom said. "Your dad

grew up in this house. He knows his way around these parts."

But Jewel and Todd *did* worry.

After lunch, I followed them up to their parents' room. The bed was made. Their parents' clothes were hung neatly in the closet. Their suitcase stood beside the closet door.

"Look." I pointed to the low table beside the bed. "Their pendants."

Jewel crossed the room and picked them up. "The pendants Tweety gave to all of us."

"I'm sure they didn't believe in them," I said. "Tweety was only trying to scare us with them—wasn't he?"

"For sure," Todd said. "One of his jokes. Mom and Dad are used to them."

"Where's *your* pendant?" Jewel asked.

I raised my hands to my neck. "I must have taken it off before I took a shower."

My mind spun. *Wait. Tweety seems to believe everything he says. Maybe he wasn't joking about the pendants.*

Todd caught the worried expression on my face. He shook his head. "You really are starting to believe Tweety's stories—aren't you?"

"The creature in the garden *wasn't* a story," I insisted. "It was real, and it attacked me."

Todd pulled out his phone. "I'll try Dad again."

This time, a bouncy ringtone sounded nearby.

Jewel followed the sound to the dresser. She pulled open the top dresser drawer and lifted out a ringing phone. She stared at it. "Dad's phone," she said. "I don't believe it. He went out without his phone."

Todd started to the bedroom door. "Put on your coat, Jewel," he said. "Let's see if we can track them."

"I'll come, too," I said. "Maybe we can find their boot prints in the snow."

Jewel ran down the hall. She returned in her coat and hat a few minutes later. "I know we shouldn't be worried," she said. "But Dad always takes his phone with him wherever he goes."

"And why didn't one of them leave us a message?" Todd said.

I zipped my parka and followed them out the back door. A swirling wind had come up, making the heavy snow fly in all directions.

Of course, I glanced into the garden first. No sign of the creature that had attacked me. The tall stalks rattled and bent in the gusting wind.

I tugged my hood over my head. But the wind blew it back down.

Jewel and Todd had their eyes lowered to the snow. "They *had* to come out the back door," Todd said. "No one ever uses the front door."

Jewel took a few steps. "They probably walked this way across the garden."

I kept my head down and scanned the snow. Jewel walked to the edge of the garden and then back. She shook her head. "I can't see their footprints. The snow is falling too fast."

Todd walked in a wide circle and ended where he started. "I don't, either," he said. "The snow must have covered them up."

Wind swirled the snow around like a tornado. A heavy blast hit me in the face. I wiped snow off my cheeks with my glove.

"We'd better go back inside," Todd said. "Mom and Dad wouldn't stay out in this storm. They'll find some-place to stay until it stops."

"And they'll be home by dinnertime," Jewel said.

But she was wrong.

13

AN IMP ARRIVES

What was going on here?

I went up to my room and sat down on the bunk. I propped my head in my hands, shut my eyes, and tried to think.

I wanted to make sense of what had happened since we'd arrived here. But I couldn't get anything to add up.

The questions kept swirling around in my head. And the answers refused to appear.

The biggest mystery was Grampa Tweety.

Were Tweety's stories about goblins and imps and strange creatures true? Did he believe them? Or did he just enjoy telling scary stories to frighten us?

What did Todd and Jewel think? They laughed at me when they thought I was taking Tweety's stories seriously.

Why did they refuse to believe me when I told them a creature jumped on me in the garden?

How could I believe that Tweety's stories were all fairy-tale fantasies after that very real creature attacked me in the garden?

I climbed to my feet and walked to the window. The wind was blowing sheets of snow against the garden wall. The shrubs and stalks all appeared to be shivering.

Did I expect the goblin to be standing down there? Maybe hunched by the dry stalks where I first saw it? Waiting? Waiting for me?

Yes, that's exactly what I expected. But there was no creature in the garden. A cold shiver ran down my back anyway.

And now there was a *new* mystery. The mystery of Mr. and Mrs. Simms.

Why did they go out for a walk without leaving a message for the kids? Without taking a phone? It was late afternoon, and they still hadn't returned.

Maybe they got lost in the snow, I thought.

But that wasn't very likely. Mr. Simms had grown up here. He had to know his way. How could he get lost?

Did Jewel and Todd's parents run into the goblin on their walk?

I had a new mission.

I had to find out the truth about the goblin. And I

had to find out if anyone here really did believe in it.

I went back to the bunk and stretched out. My head sank into the pillow. I shut my eyes and let the thoughts spin around in my mind.

I gasped when I felt a tap on my shoulder. Startled, I jerked straight up and bumped my head on the top bunk. "Oww."

I rubbed my head. Turned and stared . . . stared at . . . Stared at I-don't-know-what.

An ugly little orange guy. About two feet tall.

A little animal creature with a bald head; pointed ears; a wrinkled, whiskery face; and a pointy gray beard. He was bare chested. His orange chest was pale and smooth. He wore shorts made of long, brown leaves.

He had tiny hands, like a toddler's hands. Beneath the shorts, his legs were as thin as toothpicks. He was barefoot. And he had only two toes on each foot!

I opened my mouth to speak. But no sound came out.

He poked me with one hand. "Get up. You're in my bed." His voice was high and scratchy.

I turned and lowered my feet to the floor. "Your bed?" I finally found my voice. But my whole body was trembling.

He poked me again. Harder. "Get up. Get up. Who gave you my bed?"

I wanted to call for help, but I was trembling too hard. Was he going to hurt me? He was little—but nasty!

"Wh-who *are* you?" I stammered.

"I'm the owner of this bed!" he shouted. "It's the *imp* bed."

"Imp bed?" I cried. "You're an imp?"

"Yes, I am," he replied. He made an angry fist and waved it in my face. "Want to make something of it?"

"N-no," I stammered.

"You got a problem with me?"

"No," I repeated. "I've just never seen an imp before."

"So? Is that *my* problem?" he screamed at the top of his lungs. "Am I supposed to *cry* because you've never seen an imp before?"

"You don't have to yell," I said.

He was such an angry creature. Was he really going to fight me?

"Do you live in this house?" I asked. "Is this your room? Does Grampa Tweety know you're here?" The questions tumbled out.

He grabbed my shoulder and pinched it. His fingers were tiny but hard as steel.

"Is that *your* business?" he screamed. "Since when is my business *your* business?"

"Okay, okay," I said. I tried to shake his hand off my shoulder, but he held on tight and started to shake me.

"Wake up!" he said. "Come on. Wake up!"

"Huh? Stop shaking me."

"Wake up, Mario!"

"Hey, how do you know my name?"

I blinked a few times. Turned my head. And stared at Todd.

"Wake up, Mario. Wake up!" Todd shook me by the shoulder.

"Where's the imp?" I said.

14

BIRD FEET

"Where's the *what*?" Todd asked.

"The imp." My eyes felt heavy from sleep. I gazed around the room.

Todd laughed. "You were dreaming? Dreaming about an imp?"

I tried to blink myself alert. "I guess so."

"You're really giving me a lot of good story ideas," Todd said. "I should start making a list."

Jewel walked into the room. She wore a long, heavy wool sweater that came down almost to her knees. "Brrrr." She shivered. "It's so cold in this house. Like living in an igloo."

"Tweety says it's better for the birds," Todd said. He grinned. "Guess what Mario was dreaming about? An imp."

Jewel rolled her eyes. "Grampa Tweety really does have you under his spell."

I stood up and stretched. "It was a weird dream," I said. "The imp was very mean. He said I was in his bed. He tried to pull me out."

Todd shook his head. "Maybe tonight you'll dream about the goblin."

"Stop teasing him, Todd," Jewel scolded. "We're supposed to be having fun. Not scaring each other."

I decided to change the subject. "Is it dinnertime?"

"Almost," Jewel answered. She sighed. "And Mom and Dad aren't back."

She crossed to the window and peered out. The sky was nearly as dark as night.

"The snow is coming down so hard now," she said. "It's a blizzard. Where *are* they?"

"They'll be back by dinnertime," Todd said. "They wouldn't want to miss dinner."

Jewel spun away from the window. "Let's *do* something to take our minds off them."

"Can we explore this old house?" I said. "I haven't seen very much of it."

They exchanged glances. It took them a while to answer.

"Sounds like a plan," Todd said finally. He put a

hand on my shoulder and guided me to the bedroom door. "Maybe we'll find the room where the imps live."

"Not funny," Jewel muttered.

I followed them down the long, dimly lit hall. There were rooms on both sides of the hall. The doors were all closed. The air grew colder and smelled musty, kind of stale.

"These are mostly guest bedrooms," Todd said. "They haven't been used in a long time. Tweety and MomMom don't get many guests out here."

I tripped over a hole in the carpet. Something against the wall caught my eye. What was that? A dead mouse?

Todd and Jewel didn't see it. We turned a corner and made our way along another stretch of hallway.

Jewel stopped at a door at the end of the hall. "I know this room," she said. "I think you'll find this interesting, Mario."

She pushed the heavy door open. Then she stepped inside and fumbled on the wall till she found the light switch.

Yellow light washed over the room. Todd and I followed her in.

I saw two armchairs and a coffee table, all covered in a thick layer of dust. And then I raised my eyes to the walls—and let out a startled cry.

"What *are* those?" I asked.

"Bird feet," Todd said. "This is Grampa Tweety's memory room."

"Huh? Memory room? What's that?" I demanded.

"When one of his birds dies," Jewel started to explain, "he cuts off their feet and hangs them on the wall here. Tweety says it helps him remember every bird."

My mouth hung open as my eyes scanned the three walls. Pairs of bird feet poked out, up and down each wall. Row after row. Dozens of bird feet of all sizes covering three walls!

"I don't believe I'm seeing this," I murmured. "Walls covered in bird feet."

"I think it's kind of sweet," Jewel said.

"Sweet? It's totally weird!" I exclaimed.

"I think I agree with Jewel," Todd said. "Tweety doesn't want to part with his bird friends. So he found a way to remember them."

Jewel pointed. "Sometimes he sits in that chair and thinks about them for hours."

"But—but—" I sputtered. "He cuts off the feet.

That's—that's crazy! And what does he do with the rest of the bird? Throw it away?"

They both shrugged. "Maybe he buries it in the garden," Jewel said.

A shiver went down my back. "Can we get out of here?" I started to the door. "It's really giving me the creeps. I'll never be able to unsee this! And I know tonight I'm going to dream about birds walking around without their feet." I shivered again.

Jewel clicked off the light, and we stepped back into the hall. "What next?" Todd said.

Jewel started to the next room. "Mario, you'll like this better," she said. "It's MomMom's knitting room." She pushed open the door, and we followed her in.

My eyes went to the walls first. No bird feet sticking out in rows. Instead, I saw tall shelves with balls of yarn and other knitting and sewing materials.

An old-fashioned sewing machine stood against one wall. A wide table in the center of the room was piled high with dark green yarn. Several knitting needles poked out of the yarn. A beat-up brown leather armchair stood beside the table.

"MomMom loves to knit," Todd said. "She says she needs to keep her hands busy."

"I don't really know what she knits," Jewel said. "She's never knitted us sweaters or anything. She's never given us scarves."

"Very mysterious," I said. "All that green wool. Who does she knit things for?"

Against the back wall, the closet door was open a crack. "What's in that closet?" I asked.

Todd started to say something, but I pulled the door open quickly, peered inside—and gasped. "Hey, check this out," I said. "This is unbelievable!"

15

ROOM FOR A TAIL?

Jewel and Todd hurried over, and we gazed into the closet. We stared at the piles of knitted clothing stacked from the floor nearly to the ceiling. All made with green wool. All folded neatly.

I reached down and pulled out one of the knitted outfits. It was one piece. The top had short sleeves. Shorts at the bottom. "Is it for a kid?" I asked.

It probably would have fit us. But believe me, we would *never* wear one of these things!

Todd pulled out a few more. "They're all small," he said, holding one up in front of him. "Do you believe she knitted all these outfits?"

"You've discovered my clothing stash," a voice said behind us.

We turned to see MomMom standing in the doorway. "I love to keep my hands busy," she said, stepping into the room.

I held up an outfit. "But why are these all kid sized?" I asked.

She laughed. "I always run out of yarn. I never learn to buy enough."

She took the green outfit from me and held it up in front of her. "Look at that stitchwork. I do think I'm getting better and better." She chuckled. "When I started, I poked myself so much with the needles, I used to bleed."

"But who are these outfits for?" I asked. "For kids you know?"

"I haven't decided," she replied.

"You knit all these clothes, and you don't know who they're for?" I asked.

She handed the outfit back to me. "Do you think I'm *strange*?"

The three of us laughed. We *did* think she was strange. But we didn't want to say it.

She turned and started out of the room. "Dinner is soon. Hope you're in the mood for my newest stew."

"Have you heard from Mom and Dad?" Jewel called after her.

She was already down the hall and didn't reply.

I took one of the green outfits and stretched it

between my hands. "The wool is kind of scratchy," I said. "And wait—look!"

I held it in front of them. "There's a hole in the back of the shorts," I said. "Look. A little round hole."

I pulled out another piece of clothing. "Another one with a hole in back. Check it out. They all have holes in the back of the pants. Like for a tail!"

Todd laughed. "Room for a tail? Why would there be a hole for a tail? Think she knits these for dogs?"

Jewel grabbed the outfit away from him. She laughed. "Don't be ridiculous. She's just a very bad knitter."

"Now I'm *glad* she never sent us sweaters or pajamas or anything," Todd said.

"Can we get out of here?" I asked. "All these weird outfits are starting to freak me out."

There's something about these outfits Jewel and Todd aren't telling me, I thought. *They didn't want me to open the closet door. What is the secret here?*

"This gives me an awesome idea for a story," Todd said. "See, it's about an outfit knitted by a wizard. When you put it on, you grow a tail, and you change into a monster. And then there's no way to pull the outfit off."

"Very cool," Jewel said.

73

"I always get great ideas when I'm here," Todd said.

Jewel folded up the outfits and placed them back in the closet.

I started to the door. But I stopped when something caught my eye. Something on the table, poking out from under the pile of green wool.

I crossed to the table and shoved the wool to the side. "Check this out," I said. I was gazing at a large book with a gray cover.

I opened the cover. "It's a photo album," I said.

Jewel and Todd stepped up beside me. We turned a few pages. Each page had four or five color photos on it.

For a long time, we didn't speak. Finally, Jewel broke the silence. "No! No way!" she cried. "No way! This can't be real!"

Many of the photos seemed to have been taken at parties. Each shot was crowded—but there were no people.

No people in the photos.

I swiped through the album pages quickly.

No people. No people.

Instead, the photos all showed short, furry green creatures. Animals with long shiny cat eyes and short horns sticking up from their heads.

Most of them stood on two legs. But some were hunched on all fours.

And they all wore green, knitted outfits.

Green, knitted outfits with their furry tails poking out the back.

16

A GOBLIN GATHERING

We carried the photo album downstairs.

Grampa Tweety was filling the bird feeder at the side of the cage. Birds fluttered in midair and cheeped and squawked with excitement. Tweety snapped the feeder into place, and a dozen birds attacked it.

He turned to us. "What's up?"

Todd shoved the photo album into his arms. "These photos . . ." he said. "Tell us. What's going on here?"

"Where were the photos taken?" Jewel demanded. "Who are these weird creatures? Why are they all dressed in MomMom's outfits?"

Tweety opened the book and gazed at several pages. He closed the cover and smiled at us. "The photos aren't real," he said. "Did you think they were real?"

"They look real," Jewel said.

"They're all photoshopped," Tweety said. "The

photos are faked. Digital fakes! Can you believe it? Of course you can! You kids do this all the time."

"But, why—?" Todd started.

"Some fans of my fantasy books made this for me," Tweety said. "They gave it to me after my second book became a bestseller."

Tweety opened the cover and pointed to some words at the bottom of the page: *A Goblin Gathering.*

"These fans of mine liked the goblin chapter in my book so much, they decided to do a whole goblin book," he explained. "They put a lot of work into these photos. And I guess they did a terrific job since you thought they were real."

Did any of us believe that story?

I didn't think so.

Grampa Tweety was a storyteller. And I was pretty sure he was making all this up to explain the photo album.

How did the fans know about MomMom's knitted outfits? I wondered.

I started to ask. But MomMom shouted from the kitchen. "Dinnertime! Stew is on!"

Tweety set the album down on the couch. Then he motioned for us to follow him into the kitchen.

The tangy aroma of the stew greeted us as we took our places at the table. MomMom had baked two big loaves of bread to dunk into it.

We had a quiet dinner. No one really felt like talking. Jewel and Todd kept gazing at the empty chairs where their parents should have been sitting.

"Shouldn't we call for help?" Todd asked. "And put together a search party?"

"I'm sure they took shelter from the snowstorm," Tweety said. "I'll bet we see them back here tomorrow morning. If not, we can go searching for them then."

That didn't cheer up Todd and Jewel.

I also had a lot to think about. Thoughts that just wouldn't go away . . . the creature that attacked me in the garden . . . the murdered rabbit . . . the piles of knitted outfits with room for a tail . . . the ugly fur-covered creatures in the photo album.

So many confusing pictures in my mind.

So many questions to keep me tossing and turning in bed all night . . .

Then, the next morning, my whole world turned into a horror show.

PART TWO

17

TWEETY'S BREAKFAST

Early the next morning, I blinked myself awake. Pink morning sunlight poured into the room from the window and washed over our bunk beds.

I lowered my feet to the floor, stood up, and stretched. Todd was still asleep in the top bunk, the blanket tucked under his chin.

I pulled on jeans and a sweater and grabbed my parka. I swung the camera case over my shoulder. I was eager to see the photos I could snap on an early morning walk.

Tiptoeing silently, I made my way to the hall. I glanced into the parents' room. Mr. and Mrs. Simms were still not home.

Downstairs in the kitchen, I opened the fridge and poured myself a little cup of orange juice. Then I put on my parka and stepped out the glass doors into the backyard.

The sun was still low in the sky. It made the deep snow glow pink. I took a deep breath of the icy fresh air.

I pulled the camera from the case and held it ready in one hand. Then I began to walk, my boots crunching the snow.

I was nearing the back of the garden when I heard a cough behind me. I turned and saw Grampa Tweety entering the yard. He was bundled up in a plaid parka with a red scarf around his neck and a red wool cap pulled over his bald head.

A pair of binoculars bounced around his neck, and he was staring down at a small black book he held in his gloved hand.

He hadn't seen me. I slid behind a tall shrub. I decided I'd take a bunch of candid shots of Tweety without him knowing I was there.

I waited for him to clomp past me. Now he had his eyes on the trees up ahead. When he stepped in between the trunks, I started to follow him.

He raised his eyes to a bare tree limb. Then he began to make a gentle warbling sound. He stretched out a gloved hand.

I had my long-distance lens on the camera. I snapped a few good shots of him warbling with his head tilted up.

It didn't take long for a white dove to come floating down from the tree. The dove landed on Tweety's glove. I clicked a few more shots.

Tweety and the dove warbled at each other for a while. Then the dove fluttered back up to the tree limb.

I watched Tweety open the little black book. He pulled out a pen and wrote something down.

Maybe he keeps a diary of all the birds he's talked to, I thought.

Tweety walked deeper into the trees. He stopped in a small clearing. Then he tilted back his head and made a long whistling sound.

A few seconds later, the whistling came back from a tall evergreen shrub.

Tweety whistled again. One long whistle and two short ones.

The same sound was repeated high in the sky. And a large orange bird with a bright yellow beak swooped over Tweety's head and landed gently in front of him in the snow.

Tweety whistled. The bird whistled. Tweety wrote something in his book.

I moved behind a fat tree trunk, and I snapped away. I got several good shots of Tweety and the bird talking to each other.

Tweety tucked the book in his coat pocket and moved along a narrow path through two lines of trees. The sun was higher now, and the bright snow sparkled like silver.

I waited a minute or two and then started to follow him. He hadn't turned around. I was glad he still didn't know I was there. I wanted my photos to be a big surprise.

I swung behind a low shrub as he stopped again. He pulled off one glove and poured something into his bare hand. Birdseed?

I lifted my camera and watched as he raised his eyes and chirped at a low tree branch. Nothing happened. He chirped some more and held the hand with the seed up in front of him.

He waited. I waited.

He chirped some more.

A brown bird with speckled wings landed on the branch. It peered down at Tweety. Tweety chirped.

The bird tilted its head to one side. Then it spread its wings and fluttered down. It landed gently in Tweety's open palm and began pecking at the seeds.

I clicked a shot. Then another.

Then I stopped—and stared.

I watched Tweety cup his hands gently around the

bird. Quickly, he raised the bird to his face—and shoved the *whole bird* into his mouth.

The bird uttered one sharp squawk, but it was cut off quickly as Tweety clamped his jaws shut and began to chew. I heard the crunch of the bird's tiny bones as Tweety chewed harder.

I couldn't move. I couldn't breathe. I stared, not believing what I was seeing.

Some brown feathers poked out between Tweety's teeth as he chewed. He pushed them back into his mouth and swallowed loudly.

I couldn't help it. A startled gasp burst from my mouth.

Did he hear that?

I held my breath.

I stood perfectly still. I didn't even let myself blink.

Tweety spun around.

He looked directly at the shrub I was hiding behind.

Oh no! He SAW me!

18

NO MORE PHOTOS

I dropped to the ground behind the shrub. My camera case bounced in front of me. I lay flat as I could, my face in the snow.

I held my breath and waited for Tweety to shout my name. Or grab me.

But no. His boots crunched as he headed away from me. Whew. He hadn't seen me.

I was shaky as I climbed to my knees and lifted the camera case off the snow. I shook my head. I was so shocked, I hadn't gotten any photos of Tweety eating the bird.

No proof. No proof at all.

"What will happen if I tell Todd and Jewel?" I asked myself. "They'll laugh at me. *No way* they'll believe me."

I hid behind the tree trunk and watched Tweety march through the woods. He chirped another birdcall, and a gray bird crowed back at him from a branch overhead. Tweety pulled out his little book and wrote something in it.

Then he swung around and began walking back toward the house. I flattened myself against the tree trunk as he tromped past me. I slid around to the other side of the tree, praying he wouldn't see me, and watched him brush brown bird feathers off the front of his parka.

Then I followed him back to the house, keeping behind bushes and tall weeds. My brain was spinning so hard, I felt dizzy. The bright snow glared in my eyes.

I had to tell Todd and Jewel what I had seen. If only I had proof . . .

To my surprise, Tweety didn't go straight into the house. He stopped in the garden. I kept to the side and ducked behind some covered lawn furniture.

I almost screamed when the creature strode out from behind a low fence. I clamped my gloved hand over my mouth to muffle my cry.

Yes. The same fur-covered creature that had attacked me. It walked on two legs. About my height. Cat eyes glowing. Horns poking up from its head.

It stared at Grampa Tweety, uttered a low growl, and stopped a few feet in front of him.

I'm actually seeing this, I thought. *Tweety and the goblin. Tweety and the goblin in the garden.*

I still had my glove clamped over my mouth. My whole body was shaking—and not from the cold!

I watched Tweety reach under his plaid parka. He pulled out something green. He held it up to the grunting creature. An outfit. One of MomMom's green knitted outfits. Tweety handed it to the goblin.

It nodded to Tweety. Like it was thanking him.

Tweety turned and began walking toward the glass doors at the back of the house. I stayed behind the lawn furniture, lifted the lid on my camera case, and slid out the camera.

The creature stood against the fence. It held the green wool outfit up with two furry paws, admiring it.

Don't move, I silently begged. *Don't move.*

I had to get this shot. I had to get my proof. Now my friends would *have* to believe me.

I knew I had to hurry. I didn't even bother to raise the camera to my eye. I held the camera in front of my chest and snapped away.

Oh no.

The goblin turned quickly. Its pointed ears stood straight up beside its short horns.

It heard the camera.

The creature sniffed the air. It let out a low growl.

No. No!

It sprang toward me.

With a sharp cry, I whirled around. I gripped the camera in one hand. And ran. My boots slipped in the wet snow. I stumbled to my knees. Picked myself up. Kept running.

Was it right behind me?

Yes.

It took a big leap. Wrapped its arms around my waist. Tackled me to the snow.

I landed hard on my stomach. "Oooof." The air rushed out of my body.

The camera flew from my hand and landed several feet away on a snow-covered rock.

Struggling to catch my breath, I waited for the creature to attack.

But to my surprise, it rolled away from me. I watched it scamper on all fours to the camera.

"Hey, stop—!" I choked out as it lifted the camera in one paw.

The creature raised the camera high—and *smashed* it into the rock.

Smashed it. Again. Again.

I heard it crack. I heard the glass of the lens shatter. Jagged pieces flew over the snow.

I struggled to my feet. And watched helplessly as the creature banged the camera on the rock until it was bent and mangled and nearly flat. Eyes on me, the goblin raised its arm above its head—and heaved the camera over the garden wall.

Then, grunting loudly, it turned and came for me.

LOVEBIRDS

I struggled to force air into my lungs. My chest ached. But I lurched across the snow, my boots slipping and sliding.

The goblin let out a growl as I reached the glass doors. With trembling fingers, I fumbled with the door handle and stumbled inside.

Gasping, my chest heaving, I slid the door shut behind me.

Todd and Jewel looked up from the table where they were having breakfast.

"Mario, where were you?" Jewel demanded.

"I—I—I—" I wanted to talk, but I couldn't catch my breath. I stood there shaking.

A shrill, deafening shriek made me cry out.

And something leaped onto my chest.

"Owwww!" I fell back against the glass door. Claws dug into my skin.

"Firefly!" Todd shouted. "What is your problem?"

The cat brought his face close to mine and shrieked again. Then he jumped off me and disappeared beneath the table.

"It—it's the goblin," I choked out. "Firefly smells the goblin on me."

"Goblin?" Todd jumped to his feet. "What goblin?"

I pointed to the glass door. "It's out there. In the garden."

Jewel laughed. "You're joking, right?"

They both scooted their chairs back and hurried up beside me.

The three of us stared outside.

Nothing there.

No goblin. No creature.

I gazed at the rock where my camera had been smashed. "See the pieces of my camera out there?" I said. I tapped them both. "The goblin smashed my camera."

They squinted through the glass. "Sorry. I don't see anything," Todd said.

I stepped back and let out an angry groan. "You're really not going to believe me?"

They shook their heads.

"Well, you're *really* not going to believe what else I have to tell you!" I exclaimed. "Grampa Tweety—"

And as I said his name, he stepped into the room, followed by MomMom.

"Mario, there you are!" he said. "Where did you go?"

"I—I—I, uh, woke up early, so I went for a walk," I stammered.

"You haven't had breakfast," MomMom said. "I have a special breakfast stew on the stove. Let me dish out a bowl for you."

She sure loves to make stew!

I'd never heard of breakfast stew.

"No thanks," I said. "Not right now."

I pictured Grampa Tweety's breakfast. A feathery brown bird.

Was he looking at me suspiciously? Did he know I had followed him? That I had seen what he did?

He turned to Todd and Jewel. "I phoned the neighbors," he told them. "We're going to form a search party before lunch."

"Oh, wow. Thank goodness!" Jewel exclaimed.

"Mom and Dad must be in some kind of trouble," Todd said. "Can we come with you to look for them?"

"No need," Tweety said. "We'll be able to cover more ground without you. You two should take Mario sledding today. That will take your mind off your parents."

"I won't enjoy it," Jewel said. "I'm too worried about Mom and Dad."

"Why wait here worrying all day?" Tweety said. "When you get back, your parents will be here."

He turned to me. "Bet you've never been sledding."

"You bet right," I said.

I shivered. My clothes were wet and cold. I wanted to talk about the goblin. How it smashed my camera against a rock. I wanted to talk about Tweety shoving that bird into his mouth.

But this didn't seem like the right time. Especially with Todd and Jewel so worried about their parents.

"I'm sure your parents will turn up and be perfectly fine," MomMom said. "They probably couldn't get back because of the blizzard. But the snow has stopped. I'm going to make a special stew for them for dinner tonight."

"Mario, did you enjoy your walk?" Tweety asked. "See any birds?"

"Uh, a few," I said. I pictured him chewing and chewing.

I shivered. "I have to get out of these wet clothes. I'll be right back."

"I'll put a bowl on the table for you," MomMom said.

I walked out of the kitchen and started to the stairs. The birdcage in the living room caught my eye. I wandered over to it.

Birds fluttered and chirped excitedly as I stepped up to it. Two parakeets were digging away in the seed container.

I put my face up close and searched for the two lovebirds. They were my favorite.

I didn't see them on the low perch where they usually stood, clinging together. I raised my eyes and went up, perch by perch.

No sign of them.

I walked around to the side of the cage and searched for them from that angle. No. No lovebirds. I gazed from the ceiling down to the floor. Not there.

A frightening question flashed through my mind.

Did Tweety eat them, too?

Is that what he was doing in the cage last night?

Does he keep these birds here to EAT them?

I turned and saw Tweety standing behind me.

"Where are the lovebirds?" I asked. The words just spilled from my mouth. "I don't see them."

He squinted at me. "Lovebirds? I've never had any lovebirds."

A TERRIBLE ACCIDENT

We took old-fashioned, wooden sleds from a shed at the side of the house. They were rickety. The metal frames were rusted, and some of the wood slats were cracked and splintery.

We pulled them along the snow-covered road at the front of the house. "Are you sure these will hold us?" I asked.

"Maybe not," Todd said. "Makes it more exciting."

"Topper Hill is scary enough," Jewel said, trotting to keep up with Todd and me. "It's smooth for a short while. Then it tilts straight down."

"We've been sledding Topper Hill since we were little," Todd added. "It's awesome!"

Our breath puffed up in little white clouds in front of our faces. The snow around us shimmered red under the sun, as if it was on fire.

"I have things I want to tell you," I said.

Jewel stopped and grabbed my gloved hand. "Please, Mario," she said. "No more about the goblin."

"But—" I started.

"Jewel is right," Todd said. He fiddled with the collar of his parka. "We're worried enough about Mom and Dad. You need to take a break and stop worrying about a goblin."

Jewel sighed and kicked a clump of snow to the curb. "We're supposed to be having fun this week," she said. "Mario, why do you keep wanting to ruin it?"

"Huh? Me? Ruin it?" I cried. "Are you kidding me? I was attacked by a monster. It smashed my camera and came after me. And I'm not supposed to mention it?"

Jewel put a hand on my shoulder. "Just chill. We—"

"There's more," I said, brushing her hand away. "There's stuff about Grampa Tweety I have to tell you—"

"NO!" They both stopped and screamed.

"We know Grampa is strange," Jewel said. "But he's also so lovable."

"He's awesome," Todd said. "So is MomMom."

I stared at them. Was Tweety awesome? I was desperate to tell them how he crammed a bird into his mouth and ate it. How could I hold it inside?

Okay. I decided to save it for later. After their parents

returned. We started to trudge through the snow again, dragging our sleds.

But I had to say something. "Remember the two lovebirds in the cage in the living room?" I asked.

They both scrunched up their faces, thinking about it.

"Lovebirds?" Todd said finally. "What color are they?"

"Kind of gray with yellow feathers on their chests," I replied. "Remember them?"

They both shook their heads.

"I don't remember any lovebirds," Jewel said. "Are you sure you don't mean that gray parrot that's always biting the cage bars?"

"No. Not the parrot. The lovebirds that cling together and coo at each other."

The street started to slope up steeply. We were climbing Topper Hill.

"I don't remember them," Jewel said. "I'll have to look when we get back."

"Don't bother," I said. I tugged the rope holding the sled as the climb grew steeper. "They're not there."

Why don't they remember the lovebirds? I asked myself. *I know I didn't imagine them.*

I decided to stop thinking about everything and just focus on sledding.

We were all breathing hard when we reached the top of the hill. I gazed around, hoping to see other kids. There were boot prints and sled tracks all over the hill. But we were the only ones there now.

Low clouds floated over the sun. A wide shadow rolled over the snow, and the air grew colder. I pressed my gloves against my frozen cheeks.

I peered down to the bottom. "It's pretty steep," I said.

"Steep and fast," Todd said. "See that bump halfway down?" He pointed. "It will send you flying."

I set my sled down in front of me. "Think these old sleds will survive it?" I asked.

Jewel laughed. "Once you get going, you won't need a sled," she said. She stretched out onto her stomach on the sled. "Let's all go down at the same time. We'll show you how it works, Mario."

I lowered myself to the sled and gripped the wooden handle with both hands. Todd and Jewel were on either side of me.

"You don't even need to get a running start," Todd said. "Just ease the sled forward a few inches and—"

We were sailing down the hill, the old sleds rattling, the runners squealing. Faster. Faster. My first time on a sled was maybe the most incredible sled ride anyone ever had.

"Whoooa!" I cried out as all three of us hit the bump at the same time.

I bounced hard. The sled nearly flew out from under me. I gripped the handle, squeezing it with all my might.

The icy wind blasted my face as I started to pick up speed again. The rest of the ride down was smooth but fast as a rocket. The sled slowed as the bottom of the hill leveled out, and I rolled off it into the soft snow, laughing.

"Awesome," Jewel said. She was already on her feet. "Again. Let's go."

Todd helped me up, and we pulled our sleds back to the top of the hill. We rocketed down three more times. It was on the next trip that the terrifying accident happened.

21

IS HE ALIVE?

Icy clumps of snow had caked on Jewel's gloves. She slapped her gloves together. Then she pulled her wool cap down lower.

"Are you cold?" she asked. "I am. Maybe we should head home."

I shivered. "I'm having the best time ever!" I exclaimed. "But I think you're right." I shook the sled. "This old thing is going to fall apart any minute."

"I'm so worried about Mom and Dad," Jewel said. "I want to hurry back to the house and see if they're there."

"Well, we have to go down the hill to get home," Todd said. "One more ride. I'm going to make it a good one."

He lowered his hands to the sides of his sled, dug his boots into the snow, and pushed off. The sled was already moving fast when he jumped onto it.

Jewel and I stood side by side watching Todd rocket down the hill.

Todd screamed all the way down.

"WOOOOOHOOOO!"

But his scream cut off when the sled hit the bump.

His hands went flying off the handle. Jewel and I watched as the sled raced out from under him, speeding silently downhill.

Todd flew into the air, his hands reaching out for the sled.

He came down hard.

I heard a *craaack* as the side of his head smashed onto something hard. A rock buried under the snow?

A groan escaped Todd's open mouth. He bounced once. He came to a stop on his back. His mouth hung open, and his eyes were shut.

He didn't move.

"Nooooo!" Jewel screamed, slapping her hands to her face. "Todd? Are you okay? Todd?"

We both went running and sliding and stumbling down the hill.

My heart pounding, I dropped down beside Todd. Jewel lowered herself to the snow across from me.

Todd's eyes were still shut, and his mouth still hung open. Jewel gently shook his arm.

"Oh no. Oh noooo," she moaned. "Todd. Oh nooooo. Todd."

"Is he . . . is he b-b-breathing?" I stammered. "Jewel, is he breathing?"

IS TODD REALLY OKAY?

"We need help!" I said. But the hill was deserted. There was no one near to help us.

Jewel took Todd's hand. "Todd," she said. "Todd, can you hear me? Todd?"

His eyelids slid open. He blinked a few times, then stared up at Jewel.

"Todd?" she cried.

He groaned and turned his head from side to side. "Where's my sled?" he said.

I let out a long breath. "Huh? You're okay? Your head—?"

He pulled off his wool cap and rubbed his hair. "I'm okay," he said. He tugged the cap back on, sat up, and stretched his arms above his head.

"Your head doesn't hurt?" I asked.

"No," he answered. "Nothing hurts. I just slipped a little."

Slipped a little?

I heard his skull crack when he hit the ground.

He was totally knocked out. He didn't even seem to be breathing!

"Maybe you should stay with Todd, and I'll go get help," I said.

"Help? Why do I need help?" he said. He climbed to his feet and brushed snow off his jeans. Then he strode to the bottom of the hill and picked up his sled. "Let's go. I'll bet Mom and Dad are waiting."

How can he be perfectly fine? I asked myself. *This is too weird.*

Jewel and Todd walked on ahead of me. They were chatting calmly. The wind was blowing in my face, and I couldn't hear what they were talking about.

My thoughts were flip-flopping. It didn't seem possible, but things were getting stranger and stranger . . .

I needed Todd and Jewel to help me figure things out. And I wanted to show them what I'd found out about Grampa Tweety.

I trotted to catch up with them. "I have a plan for tomorrow," I said. "I want you two to get up real early with me and go for a walk before breakfast."

A SPY MISSION

Early the next morning, the sun was just rising over the snowy ground when I woke up. I climbed to the top bunk and shook Todd awake.

He groaned. "Give me a break." He turned on his side. "One more hour."

I shook him some more. "Get up. There's something you have to see."

He groaned again and sat up, rubbing his eyes. "I was having such a nice dream. I dreamed my parents were back and—"

"They're not back yet," I said. "I checked their room. But they'll be back. Everyone's sure of it."

Todd pulled on jeans and a sweatshirt, and we went down the hall to wake up Jewel. She was already dressed, brushing her hair in front of the dresser mirror.

"What's the point of this?" she demanded. "Why couldn't we wait till after breakfast?"

"We're going to do some spying," I said. "There's something you need to see. If I told it to you, you wouldn't believe me. So I want you to see it with your own eyes."

She frowned at me. "Couldn't I see it with my own eyes after breakfast?"

We started down the stairs. I raised a finger to my lips, motioning for them to be very quiet.

"Who are we spying on?" Todd whispered.

"You'll see," I whispered back.

We crept through the kitchen and out the glass doors. A gentle wind was blowing, sending the powdery snow sailing in all directions.

I lowered my gaze to the snow. Yes! I saw fresh boot prints leading away from the house. Grampa Tweety must be on his morning walk in the woods.

"Follow me," I said.

Nothing moved in the garden. We walked through it, our boots digging into the soft snow. High above us, some birds flew by silently, shadows against the clouds.

In the distance, I could see Tweety in his plaid parka, entering the woods. Todd and Jewel saw him, too.

Todd stepped in front of me to stop me. "Mario, are we spying on Grampa Tweety?" he demanded. "Why?"

"You'll see," I said.

"He's going on his morning bird watch," Jewel said. "Why on earth would we want to spy on that?"

"You'll see," I repeated.

They both stared hard at me. I knew they wanted to turn around and go back to the warm house, but I had to convince them to stay.

"You have to trust me," I said. "I know this is weird. But you'll understand in a few minutes."

"Shouldn't we run up and join him?" Jewel demanded.

"No. No way!" I cried. "There's going to be a surprise. I promise. Just don't let him see you."

They exchanged glances. Then they finally agreed. We began trudging through the snow again.

I kept my eyes on Tweety up ahead.

And I couldn't help but think: *What if he doesn't do it this morning?*

What if he doesn't have a bird breakfast?

What if he just does a normal bird-watching thing? And there's nothing interesting for us to see?

What will Jewel and Todd think of me dragging them out of bed for nothing?

Will they ever believe me again?

BREAKFAST

The three of us stayed close to the low bushes. They were covered in fat thorns, and a thorn poked my hand right through my glove.

"Oww—" I started to let out a cry from the sharp pain. But I caught myself and stopped.

Todd and Jewel were staring at me. "Are you okay?" Todd whispered.

I nodded and rubbed my hand. "Watch out for thorns."

I turned my eyes to Tweety, who was wandering through the trees up ahead. Had he heard my cry?

No.

He was chirping up at a tree limb.

We ducked behind the shrub and watched.

A robin appeared on a low branch. It puffed its red breast out and chirped back at Tweety.

Tweety made a note in his little book. Then he moved along the line of trees.

I heard a rustling in the snow behind us. I spun around and saw a huge, fat bird trudging slowly through the snow, its head bobbing as it walked.

"Is that a pheasant?" I whispered.

Todd and Jewel shook their heads. "It's a wild turkey," Todd said.

"Comical looking, isn't it?" Jewel whispered. "It's so big. It's hard to believe it can fly."

Bobbing its head, the turkey strutted in a straight line, turned, and headed away from us.

We swung around to watch Grampa Tweety.

He stopped in front of a snow-covered tree that was tilted to one side. It looked about to topple over. A tiny red bird perched on one of its limbs.

Tweety stepped closer to the bird.

Is he going to eat it?

At my sides, Todd and Jewel watched in silence.

Tweety and the little bird had a chirping conversation. They chirped back and forth at each other. Then the little bird fluttered off the limb and vanished into the trees.

Tweety wrote something in his book.

Todd bumped me with his elbow. "This is boring," he whispered.

Jewel shivered. "I'm too cold, Mario. This is a waste of time."

I raised a finger to my lips. "Just keep watching," I whispered. "We'll go back soon. Promise."

Tweety tucked the little book into the back pocket of his pants. He stepped up to a low tree branch. He removed something from another pocket and poured it into his glove.

Birdseed.

He sent a series of long tweets up to the tree.

Is this it? I wondered. *Is he about to have a bird for breakfast?*

Todd and Jewel huddled at my sides.

I squinted hard and watched a gray-feathered bird flutter into Tweety's gloved hand. The bird lowered its head and began to peck at the seed.

Yes. Yes!

Tweety wrapped his other glove over the back of the bird. He covered the bird with his glove and lifted it higher.

The little bird let out a sharp squeal as Tweety ripped

off its legs and tossed them away. Then he stuffed the whole bird into his mouth and began to chew.

"Do you see?" I cried to Todd and Jewel. "That's what I wanted you to see. Do you see?"

"See *what*?" Todd said.

HOW CAN I PROVE IT TO THEM?

"What Tweety just did!" I cried. "Didn't you see—"

"Sorry," Jewel said. "We were watching *them*!"

She pointed to a line of wild turkeys behind us, maybe six or seven of them, trotting in a line.

"It's like a wild turkey parade," Todd said. "Too bad you don't have your camera."

"But—but—but—" I sputtered.

I turned back. Tweety was brushing feathers off the front of his parka. Then he spun away from the trees and started to walk back toward the house.

"Y-y-you missed it," I stammered. "You missed the whole thing." I shook my head. "I don't have words . . ."

Jewel shook my shoulder. "What is it? What did you want to show us, Mario?"

"Your grandfather just ate a bird!" I exclaimed.

They both burst out laughing.

"No. Seriously," Todd said when he finally stopped.

"Why did you drag us out here? What did you want to show us?"

"I—I—I—" I balled my gloved hands into fists. "Forget it," I muttered.

How could they turn away at just the right moment?

I sighed. "Let's go back and have breakfast."

The wild turkeys followed us for a while as we walked back to the house.

Something is very wrong here, I told myself. *Grampa Tweety is not the kind old man he seems to be.*

There really is a vicious goblin in the garden—and Tweety knows about it.

I have to prove it to them.

Their parents could be in real danger.

We could ALL be in real danger.

But . . . how? How can I prove it?

That afternoon, I had the answer.

GREMLINS

We headed into the house for breakfast. No sign of Todd and Jewel's parents at the breakfast table. I saw the disappointed looks on my friends' faces.

Grampa Tweety was already at his place at the table. He motioned for us to sit down. "Nice to see you kids getting fresh air in the morning," he said. "I had a good walk, too. See any interesting birds?"

Like the one you chewed up and swallowed?

"Just some wild turkeys," Todd answered.

MomMom was dishing out bowls of steaming hot porridge.

Jewel slid into her place. "No word about Mom and Dad?" she asked.

Tweety shook his head. "The neighbors and I are going to keep searching after breakfast. I'm sure they took shelter somewhere."

"But the snowstorm has been over for ages," Todd said. "Why wouldn't they just come home?"

"Not to worry. They're probably just snowed in," MomMom said. "Now, eat your porridge while it's hot. It's good for your bones."

Tweety slurped a few big spoons of porridge. "Mario gave me a good idea," he said, smiling at me. "He mentioned lovebirds. I forgot how much I adore lovebirds. I'm definitely going to buy some for the cage real soon."

"Mario mentioned lovebirds to us, too," Todd said. He turned to me. "Guess you have lovebirds on your mind."

"Guess so," I muttered. I didn't know what else to say.

Tweety turned to Todd. "Have you written anything lately? You know I love reading your stuff. I like to think you're following in my footsteps. I'm really impressed with your fantasy stories."

Todd swallowed some big lumps of porridge, then wiped his mouth with his napkin. "Well . . . I have this idea for a story about a gremlin," he said. "But I have to do the research first."

Tweety chuckled. "Research? You don't have to do research. I can tell you about gremlins."

"You've studied gremlins?" Todd asked.

"No need to study them," Tweety replied. "I ran into a few of them last month!"

I set down my spoon. *Here comes another story,* I thought. *Will it be true—or made up?*

Tweety leaned over the table, his eyes on Todd. "I was having truck trouble, see," he started. "Sure, the truck was old. But it wasn't *that* old. And I couldn't figure out why sometimes it refused to start. And sometimes it acted like it didn't want to pick up speed."

"Did you take it to a garage?" Todd asked.

Tweety nodded. "Truth is, I don't know anything about cars or trucks, even though I've been driving since I was twelve. Around here in the wilderness you can't get anywhere unless you drive. So you start early! Anyway, I almost never looked under the hood or learned anything about how cars work."

He scooped up some more porridge, wiped his mouth, and continued the story. "One morning it took me forever to get the truck to start. I thought I might have to have it towed. But it finally kicked over, and I drove it to Hurley's Fix-It in Andover Plains."

He shook his head. "Believe me, it was a long ride. I was flooring the gas pedal, and I couldn't get it to go over thirty."

"What happened when you got it to the garage?" Todd asked.

"I pulled it up to the service dock, and Hurley came walking over," Tweety said. "I told him the problems I was having, and he said let's take a look under the hood.

"So, he pops the latch and starts to raise the hood. And that's when it got weird."

We all stared at Tweety. No one said a word, waiting for him to tell us what was weird.

"Hurley was pulling up the hood," Tweety said. "And a hand reached out and pulled the hood back down."

"No way!" I cried. "A hand reached out from under the hood?"

Tweety nodded. "A slender green hand with only three fingers. It stretched out from the engine and tugged the hood down. Hurley and I both let out cries. Hurley grabbed the hood again and began to raise it. And again, this three-fingered green hand on a skinny green arm reached out and closed the hood."

Tweety took a long sip of coffee. "Hurley was shaking his head and muttering under his breath, totally confused. But, of course, I knew what it was."

He waited for someone to ask.

"What was it?" Jewel said finally.

"A gremlin," Tweety answered. "I had a gremlin living in the engine of my car, and he didn't want to be disturbed."

"Well, what did you do?" Todd asked. "How did you get him out?"

"I couldn't," Tweety replied. "You can't get a gremlin to do something he doesn't want to do."

"But didn't Hurley—?" Jewel started.

"Hurley and I got the hood open finally," Tweety continued. "The gremlin had made a nice bed for himself out of grass and sticks and leaves. We tried to reason with him. But gremlins are mischievous. He just pretended he didn't understand us. *No way* he would leave his comfortable home in my truck."

Tweety was sure enjoying telling us this story. But it couldn't be true—*could* it?

"Believe it or not, we found two more gremlins living under the truck bed," Tweety said. "They giggled and tittered and slapped their bony green knees and hooted at us. They were having the best time.

"Hurley got all red in the face and said he couldn't deal with this. He went inside his garage. And that was that."

"But how did you get rid of them?" I asked.

Tweety squinted at me. "Get rid of gremlins? You're

joking, right? I couldn't. I gave them the truck, and Hurley drove me home."

We all gazed at Tweety in silence.

He laughed. "Don't stare at me. You want to see the truck? Go to Andover Plains. Hurley says the gremlins drive it up and down Main Road all day long."

Todd shook his head. "Awesome story, Grampa," he said. "Is it okay if I use some of it in my gremlin story?"

"Not a story," Tweety muttered. "All my stories are true."

I finished the porridge. It was so thick and heavy, my stomach felt as if I'd swallowed cement.

I went upstairs to my room to take off my sweater.

Tweety and his stories, I thought. *Now he wants us to believe that gremlins took his truck. And this guy Hurley didn't even think it was strange. Wow.*

I pulled the sweater over my head and started to toss it onto my bottom bunk. But I stopped when something caught my eye.

Something on my pillow. Small and bright green.

Squinting at it, I walked over to the bed and picked it up.

A tiny green glove. With only three fingers.

27

GOBLIN MONDAY

It was Monday afternoon. I decided I needed to get out of the house and think. My belly still felt like a rock from the breakfast porridge. I needed exercise.

The fresh, cool air made me feel better instantly. The sunlight on the snow made everything gleam.

I started to cross the garden when I saw that the shed door stood open. One of the sleds we had used had toppled out.

I picked up the sled and stood it up against the other two. I had trouble latching the shed door, but I finally got it locked.

I was nearly out of the garden when I saw the goblin.

I froze. My gloved hands tightened into fists at my sides, ready for a fight. My breath caught in my throat.

Of course, I didn't have my camera. The creature had wrecked it.

He stared back at me with those cat eyes, grunting

softly. The pointed ears poked up sharply beside the dark horns.

This was my chance. My chance to prove to Todd and Jewel that the creature was real!

I thought about shouting for them to come see it. But they might not hear me, and the creature would run off.

Standing on two legs, it took a heavy step toward me. Then another. The grunting grew into growls.

I moved quickly. I tore the canvas covering off the lawn chair in front of me. Then I dove forward—

Leaped at the growling creature—

And tossed the cover over its head.

Gasping for breath, my heart thudding in my chest, I wrapped it around the goblin. Pulled it tight.

"Gotcha!" I screamed.

FRIENDS?

I gasped when the creature slid out from the bottom of the canvas bag and dropped to the ground. It hit the snow on its belly.

"No! Oh noooo!" I cried.

I watched it scramble away on all fours. I stood there holding the empty cover.

The goblin spun around to face me, rising up on its hind legs. Eyes wide with anger, it snapped its jaws loudly. Grunting, chest heaving, it lowered itself to attack.

What could I do? I couldn't outrun it. The canvas cover was useless. I tossed it aside.

No time to think. No time to make any kind of plan.

I lowered my shoulder like a football running back. I dug my boots into the snow and dove at the creature again.

Running hard, I jammed my shoulder into its belly.

Its mouth flew open in a sharp cry of surprise.

Wrapping my arms around it, I tackled it and brought it to the ground.

The goblin was so surprised, it didn't put up much of a fight. I slid off it and climbed to my knees.

It put up a weak struggle as I grabbed its front paws and tugged them behind it. Then I used all my strength to pull the creature to its feet.

Grunting angrily, the goblin tried to twist out of my grasp. But I held on tight and shoved it toward the glass doors.

The goblin squirmed and struggled. Its tail slapped back and forth, trying to bat me away.

I butted the goblin's back with my head. Slid open the door. Pushed it into the house.

"Hey—!" I tried to call out. But my voice was weak from my struggle. "Where is everyone?" No one heard me. I could only whisper.

The goblin tugged hard and almost escaped my grasp.

"No! No! You're not getting away!" I choked out. I tightened my hands around its wrists.

I gazed frantically around the kitchen. No place to stow the creature while I found the others. And then the broom closet near the hall caught my eye.

"Yes!"

I gave it another hard shove.

The goblin let out an angry growl.

Don't panic, I told myself. *You've got him. You've got him. You're almost there.*

With strength I didn't know I had, I pushed the creature into the narrow closet. I slammed the door shut. My hand trembled on the latch. But I slid it closed. And backed away, struggling to breathe.

Thud, thud, thud . . .

The goblin pounded on the other side of the door. It sounded like booms of thunder. I knew the door wouldn't hold long.

"Hey—where is everyone?" I shouted.

I ran into the living room, startling the birds in the big cage and sending them fluttering up and down.

I raced to the stairs. Grampa Tweety was halfway down. "Mario, what's all the shouting about?" he called.

"I've got it!" I cried. "I captured it!"

"You *what*?" Tweety's eyes went wide. His face darkened to red.

Jewel and Todd were right behind him. I led them into the kitchen. The goblin was still pounding on the broom closet door.

"Uh-oh . . ." Tweety's face grew even darker.

I stared at him. "*You* know the goblin really exists," I said. "I saw you with it. I saw you with it in the garden."

He opened his mouth to answer me but then just shook his head.

I turned to Jewel and Todd. "You both laughed at me," I said. "But now I have proof. The goblin is real. I caught it and dragged it into this closet."

They didn't say anything. Grampa Tweety's chest was heaving up and down, and he was breathing noisily.

Was he scared? Was he nervous? Angry?

I grabbed the latch and slid it open. The door crashed against the wall as the goblin burst out of the closet.

The creature stopped in front of us, snarling and snapping its jaws. Its eyes went from me to Grampa Tweety.

No one moved. It was a frightening staring match.

And then Tweety slapped his forehead and sighed. "What have you done?" he cried. "Mario, what have you done?"

"Huh?" I replied. "What have I done? I've captured the goblin."

"But—but—" Tweety sputtered. "You—you can't! You can't! Don't you realize the goblin has *friends*?"

And just as he said that, there was a hard knock on the front door.

29

"ARE THEY GOING TO TEAR US APART?"

MomMom stepped into the room, carrying a big, empty metal stewpot.

There was more heavy pounding on the front door.

"Do we have company?" she asked Grampa Tweety. Then her mouth dropped open when she saw the goblin standing in front of us. The stewpot dropped from her hands and clanged to the floor.

"Oh no," MomMom groaned. "I don't believe it." She pressed her hands to her face.

Heavy *thuds* at the front door. It sounded as if someone was trying to kick the door open.

"Don't answer it!" The words burst from my mouth.

"We don't need to," Tweety said.

I heard a cracking sound. A crash. Banging footsteps. We hurried to the living room.

Another goblin stood staring at us. Behind it, the front door lay splintered on its side.

This goblin was short, shorter than me. Its fur was reddish orange. It tapped the floor with black hooves on its hind legs.

I gasped when I realized it was wearing one of MomMom's knitted green outfits.

What is up with that?

The goblin had a long tail like a horse's tail. It poked out from the back of the knitted shorts. The tail swept back and forth over the floor as the creature gazed at us one at a time.

The goblin I had caught rushed past us to greet its friend. They bumped chests and grunted a greeting at each other.

"Only one!" Jewel cried.

But then we heard the glass doors in the kitchen crash open.

The air filled with grunts and growls and shuffling footsteps.

Four more fur-covered goblins burst into the room. They were all wearing green knitted outfits. They greeted the two others with grunts and chest bumps.

I backed up against the living room wall. My legs were quivering like rubber bands, and my head throbbed and felt about to explode. I had to force myself to breathe.

I'm in the middle of a horror movie!

What are they going to do? Are they going to tear us apart?

Todd and Jewel backed up now until they were on either side of me. Their eyes were wide. They stared without blinking at the grunting creatures that filled the room.

The birds in the big cage were in a total panic. Their frightened squawks drowned out the grunts and growls of the goblins.

Birds fluttered to the top of the cage, then dropped down to the floor. Birds threw themselves against the cage bars and crashed into one another. The cage was filled with flying feathers.

My two friends and I huddled close together and watched as the goblins formed a tight line in front of us. They snapped their jaws and tapped the floor as if eager to attack us.

Tweety and MomMom stood at the side of the room, mouths hanging open. I saw Tweety grab MomMom's hand and squeeze it.

Moving together, the creatures took a step toward us.

Fear choked my throat. My knees started to fold.

I turned to the grandparents. "MomMom—Grampa Tweety—" I choked out, my voice cracking. "Help us. Aren't you going to do anything to help us?"

"We can't," Tweety replied.

30

TWO MORE GOBLINS

Why are the grandparents just standing there? Why can't they help us?

Why are the goblins wearing clothes that MomMom knitted?

What are the goblins planning?

Is there any way to survive this? Any way at all?!

The questions flew through my mind, too fast to think of any answers.

The goblins tightened their line. They were hunched shoulder to shoulder. They moved closer to us, one step at a time. One slow step. Then another.

A terrified scream rose up from my throat. But I forced it down and turned to Tweety again. "Help us—please!"

"I can't," he said again.

And a few seconds later, I knew why.

I saw pointy ears and two stubby horns pop up on

top of his bald head. The ears stood straight up like wolf ears. Green fur grew over his face. And his eyes narrowed to dark cat eyes.

Tweety let go of MomMom's hand, and I saw a green paw at the end of his arm.

Tweety squatted up and down a few times, testing out his goblin legs. Then he began to grunt. A purple tongue slid from his mouth and licked his lips.

And beside him, MomMom changed, too.

"Yaw, yaw, yawwww!" She opened her mouth wide in a strange animal howl. *"Yaw, yaw, yawwww!"*

As she changed into a goblin, Tweety took up the howl. *"Yaw, yaw, yawwww!"*

The two of them howled at the ceiling, and in seconds they had turned completely from their human shape . . . into howling goblins.

"Oh noooo!" The scream finally escaped my throat.

But it was drowned out by the line of goblins who picked up the shrill howl. And now the deafening wails rang out from around us, ringing off the high ceiling and the living room walls.

"Yaw, yaw, yawwww!"

"Yaw, yaw, yawwww!"

"Yaw, yaw, yawwww!"

The birds squawked and slammed into each other. Feathers flew into the room.

A goblin reached out and pulled me toward him.

"No—please!" I cried. I tried to tug myself free, but the goblin was too strong.

I dragged my heels on the floor. But the creature didn't stop until it had forced me into the center of the living room. Then they all formed a circle around me. I saw MomMom and Tweety join the circle.

"*Yaw, yaw, yawwww!*"

"*Yaw, yaw, yawwww!*"

They moved to the right. Then they stopped and moved the circle to the left. A strange dance. The creatures moved together, tightening the circle around me and howling.

Around and around. They all kept their eyes on me as they did their frightening dance.

I raised both hands in front of me. "Please! Stop!" I cried in a shrill, high-pitched voice. "Please! What are you going to do to me?"

To my surprise, the goblins did stop. They all stood still.

I heard a noise at the front door.

I turned—in time to see Mr. and Mrs. Simms step into the room.

"Mom! Dad! You're back!" Todd cried.

"Oh, thank goodness!" I gushed. "Can you help us? Can you do something—"

I cut myself short. My breath caught in my throat.

Mr. and Mrs. Simms were barefoot.

And . . . and . . . they didn't have feet.

They had hooves.

31

THEY'VE SEEN TOO MUCH!

"Sorry we can't help you," Mr. Simms said in a gruff voice. It sounded like he had broken glass in his throat. "We were trapped in the snow, and our goblin friends helped dig us out. We have to be loyal to the goblins."

Mrs. Simms lowered her head and grunted softly.

"Goblins . . . all goblins," I muttered.

I saw that Grampa Tweety and MomMom had changed back into their human bodies. Todd and Jewel stood silently, pressed against the wall.

The goblins still surrounded me in their circle. They didn't move. They had their eyes on Tweety, waiting for him to tell them what to do.

The room grew silent except for the bird cries from the birdcage.

It was like somebody had pushed PAUSE.

I stared hard at the ring of goblins. Could I break

through their circle and make a run for it? If I did escape somehow, where would I go?

Tweety groaned and shook his head. "The three of them have seen too much," he said. "You can't take them home. We really have no choice."

Can't take us home?

"Wh-what are you going to do?" I stammered.

He stared hard at me, and then at Jewel and Todd. Then he motioned with one hand to the goblins. "Lock them in the birdcage. I know what to do with them."

32

THEY WON'T HELP THEIR OWN KIDS!

The goblins moved in quickly. They grabbed the three of us and began to force us toward the cage.

I turned to Mr. and Mrs. Simms. "These are your kids!" I cried. "Aren't you going to do anything?"

Mrs. Simms kept her head down. Her husband muttered something and turned his face away.

They're not going to help their own kids!

One of the goblins gave me a hard shove. I stumbled forward, struggling to stay on my feet.

Another goblin tore open the cage door. Two more goblins shoved Todd and Jewel into the cage. They didn't scream or cry or try to fight. I think they were in total shock.

Birds fluttered and squawked. A bluebird landed on Todd's head, and he didn't even move to brush it away.

A goblin pushed me up to the open cage door. I suddenly had an idea.

I spun around to face the creature.

136

I reached under my shirt. "The pendant!" I shouted to Grampa Tweety. "I'm wearing the pendant!"

I tugged it out and raised it in front of me.

Tweety had given us all pendants to protect us. He said they were filled with nutmeg. And the aroma would put the goblins to sleep.

I pushed the pendant into the goblin's face. The creature stared blankly at me and didn't back up.

"That won't help you, Mario," Tweety said, taking a few steps closer. "I was just messing with you."

"What?" I cried, gripping the pendant with all my strength. "What? The pendant . . . the nutmeg . . . ?"

Tweety chuckled. "Sniff it."

I raised it to my nose and inhaled. A sigh escaped my throat. "Smells like cinnamon," I murmured.

"You got that right," Tweety said. "They're filled with cinnamon. Not nutmeg."

"Why?" I cried. "Why did you give them to us?"

"Messing with you," Tweety repeated. "I guess I have a weird sense of humor."

"But—but—" I sputtered.

"Enough talk," Tweety snapped. "I'm sorry, Mario. But you've seen too much. We have to protect ourselves. I can't let you go home."

He motioned to the goblin. "Push him into the cage."

The goblin burst forward quickly and shoved me into the cage. I stumbled into some birds, who squawked and fluttered.

I brushed them away with both arms. Grabbed the cage door before the goblin could close it. Pushed against it as hard as I could—and broke free.

With a cry, I ripped the pendant off my neck. And I heaved it into the goblin's face.

He let out a squeal of surprise. The metal pendant hit his eye. He reached up to rub it.

It was all the time I needed.

I ducked under him and took off running.

The other goblins turned to chase me. But I was already racing free.

And I knew exactly where I was going.

33

NUTMEG?

I reached the staircase and started racing up the steps two at a time.

Were the goblins coming after me? I heard the rumble of heavy thuds on the floor. I didn't stop to look back.

As I ran, I heard Mr. Simms yelling at Todd and Jewel. "Todd, I knew we shouldn't have brought your friend." His voice was gruff. He growled the words.

"He's not *my* friend!" I heard Todd reply. "He's Jewel's friend!"

"No, he isn't!" Jewel cried. "I thought *you* invited him, Todd!"

"No way!" Todd exclaimed.

"Then who invited him?"

Their voices faded as I reached the second-floor landing. Breathing hard, I flew into my bedroom and darted to the closet. I tugged open the closet door and reached down for the tool I always carry with me.

The leaf blower.

Gripping it tightly, I raised it to my chest. Then I headed for the steps to return to the living room.

The goblins stood bunched at the bottom of the stairs. Ready to capture me when I came down. They began to snarl the minute they saw me.

I raised the leaf blower and pointed it at them.

"Mario? The leaf blower?" Todd shouted from inside the cage. "What are you going to do with that?"

"Give up, Mario. You can't hurt anyone with a leaf blower," Grampa Tweety growled.

"Sorry to ruin your day," I said. "But it's filled with nutmeg. Say goodnight, everyone!"

I aimed the nozzle into the crowd of goblins—and blasted away.

Would it work?

34

MY SECRET IDENTITY

The nutmeg shot out in a pale brown cloud. It misted over the goblins like a blowing fog.

Now half-goblin, half-human, Tweety and MomMom came rushing at me. I turned the nozzle—and covered them in nutmeg spray.

Choking, the goblins batted the air with their paws. Trying to force the nutmeg cloud away. Then, grabbing their throats, they dropped to their knees, coughing and gagging.

One by one, their eyes closed, and they sprawled flat on the floor. Tweety and MomMom had fallen on their backs, green fur-covered arms outstretched. I watched their eyes close. They didn't move.

I tugged open the cage door. Birds came flying out, eager to escape. They chirped and squawked and darted back and forth along the living room ceiling.

Todd and Jewel stepped out of the cage. Their eyes were wide. They stared at me without speaking. I could see they were still in shock.

Mr. and Mrs. Simms stood quietly and watched. Their hooves were gone. They had changed back to human form.

I raised the leaf blower. Did they plan to attack me?

"What about us?" Mr. Simms finally spoke. "What are you going to do with us?"

"Are you going to knock us out, too?" Mrs. Simms said in a trembling voice. "Please—"

"No," I said. "I need you to drive us home."

Of course, I didn't trust them. I kept the leaf blower aimed at them.

"Help me lock these goblins in the birdcage," I told them, "and I'll let you drive us home."

Mr. and Mrs. Simms exchanged glances. "Okay," she said. "Okay. We can do that."

I lowered the leaf blower. "I was assigned to capture goblins in Vermont," I said. "I had no idea YOU were the goblins! Guess I got real lucky."

They both uttered cries of surprise. "I don't get this," Mr. Simms said, squinting at me. "Assigned to capture goblins? *Assigned?* Who *are* you?"

I pulled a business card from my pocket and handed it to him.

He raised it between him and his wife and read it:

MARIO GALAGOS, Agent, United Goblin Hunters.

"WHAT'S SO FUNNY?"

"Mario, how long have you been a goblin hunter?" Jewel asked.

"Actually," I told her, "this was my first assignment."

We were sitting in the back of the Simms family SUV. I was wedged in the back seat between Todd and Jewel.

We were on the highway leading to the Simmses' home, passing tall pine trees and snow-covered fields.

The parents had been silent for most of the trip. But now, Mr. Simms spoke up.

"What's going to happen to my parents? What are you going to do to Grampa Tweety and MomMom?" he asked. He had eyes on me in the rearview mirror.

"I called some other agents to pick them up," I said. "And the other goblins, too."

Mrs. Simms shook her head. She sighed. "It's so sad."

"I know," I replied. "But I'm sure you know the

United States has strict laws against goblins. That's why the agency was formed. To find them and round them up."

A large oil truck rumbled past us. Our SUV shook from side to side.

"I had you fooled," I told them. "No one ever suspects that a kid is an agent."

"What about my wife and me?" Mr. Simms asked.

"I'm letting you drive us home," I told him. "But you will have to be captured after we get there. I'm really sorry. But I have no choice."

We drove on in silence for a while. The sun kept disappearing behind high clouds that drifted by, sending long shadows over the fields.

I suddenly realized that both Jewel and Todd were grinning at me.

"What's so funny?" I asked.

They both chuckled. "Well . . ." Jewel started. "Mario, you forgot one thing."

"Huh?" I said. "What did I forget?"

"You really are a beginner," Todd said. "You forgot that our parents are goblins . . . *And that makes us goblins, too!*"

"Whoa! Wait!" I cried.

I watched the fur grow on their faces. Talons poked out from their fur-covered paws. Their breathing changed to sharp grunts.

Todd squeezed my leg.

"Stop! Please! Wait!" I cried. I tried to move. But I was trapped between them.

Jewel brought her face close and snapped her jaws.

Todd dug his talons into my leg.

"No! Please, noooooo!" I screamed.

Jewel sank her teeth into my chest.

Growling, Todd chewed on my arm.

Then he tossed his head back and laughed.

"Yaaaay!" he cheered. "Best winter break EVER!"

And they all burst out laughing.

ABOUT THE AUTHOR

R.L. Stine says he gets to scare people all over the world. So far, his books have sold more than 400 million copies, making him one of the most popular children's authors in history. The Goosebumps series has more than 150 titles and has inspired a TV series and two motion pictures. R.L. Stine himself is a character in the movies! He has also written the teen series Fear Street, which has been adapted into three Netflix movies, as well as other scary book series. His newest picture book for little kids, illustrated by Marc Brown, is titled *Why Did the Monster Cross the Road?* R.L. Stine lives in New York City with his wife, Jane, a former editor and publisher. You can learn more about him at rlstine.com.

Read on for a creepy sneak peek of
Night of the Living Mummy!

HOW TO MUMMIFY A PERSON

I pointed to the three-pronged tool in the photo on my laptop screen. Kids in the back rows of the classroom leaned forward to see it better.

"This is what the ancient Egyptians used to pull the brain out of the skull," I said.

A few kids groaned. I heard my friend Jayden laugh. Jayden laughs at just about everything.

Mr. Horvat, our science teacher, stepped in front of the laptop and studied the photo. "Happy, can you explain how the tool was used?" he asked.

I knew the answer. I know everything about ancient Egypt. It's not like I'm obsessed or anything. I just have a thing about ancient Egypt. And mummies.

I actually dream about living in ancient Egypt and walking around the pyramids. And I dream about mummies. But the dreams aren't nightmares. Like I'm not screaming and running because a mummy is staggering after me, trying to grab me.

My cousin Abby says it's easy to explain. She says it's because my mom is a paleontologist. That's a scientist who digs up ancient things like dinosaur bones. Abby says I dream about ancient Egypt because I want to be like my mom. Abby knows me pretty well. We see each other a lot because we're in the same class in school.

Jayden says I'm just weird.

He's probably right.

I pointed again to my laptop screen. "Here's what they did when they wanted to mummify someone," I said. "They slid this tool up the dead person's nose. They pushed it up until it reached the brain. Then they pulled the brain out through the nose."

Rena Graham in the front row made a loud gagging sound. She jumped up with a sick look on her face and ran out of the room, holding her hand over her mouth. Rena has a very sensitive stomach.

Other kids were groaning and moaning. Jayden was laughing.

"They had to clean out the body before they dipped it in burning tar," I said.

"Make him stop!" a kid in the back yelled.

Mr. Horvat stepped in front of the laptop before I could show the burning tar photo. "I think that's enough for now, Happy," he said. "Some of your classmates are feeling a little queasy." He chuckled. "I know *I* am." He burped into his hand.

"Mummifying someone was a difficult process," I said. "And pretty gross. I guess that's why a lot of people today are afraid of mummies."

"I think the movies about mummies coming to life are at fault," the teacher said. "Some of those movies are terrifying." He shivered.

"I *wish* mummies could come to life," I said. "Wouldn't it be awesome to actually talk to someone who lived in ancient Egypt?"

Of course, when I said that, I had no idea what a terrible wish that was.

Goosebumps
HOUSE OF SHIVERS

#1: *Scariest. Book. Ever.*

#2: *Goblin Monday*

#3: *Night of the Living Mummy*

Goosebumps

The original bone-chilling series!

- ☐ NIGHT OF THE LIVING DUMMY
- ☐ DEEP TROUBLE
- ☐ MONSTER BLOOD
- ☐ THE HAUNTED MASK
- ☐ ONE DAY AT HORRORLAND
- ☐ THE CURSE OF THE MUMMY'S TOMB
- ☐ BE CAREFUL WHAT YOU WISH FOR
- ☐ SAY CHEESE AND DIE!
- ☐ THE HORROR AT CAMP JELLYJAM
- ☐ HOW I GOT MY SHRUNKEN HEAD
- ☐ THE WEREWOLF OF FEVER SWAMP
- ☐ A NIGHT IN TERROR TOWER
- ☐ WELCOME TO DEAD HOUSE
- ☐ WELCOME TO CAMP NIGHTMARE
- ☐ GHOST BEACH
- ☐ THE SCARECROW WALKS AT MIDNIGHT
- ☐ YOU CAN'T SCARE ME!
- ☐ RETURN OF THE MUMMY

- ☐ REVENGE OF THE LAWN GNOMES
- ☐ PHANTOM OF THE AUDITORIUM
- ☐ VAMPIRE BREATH
- ☐ STAY OUT OF THE BASEMENT
- ☐ A SHOCKER ON SHOCK STREET
- ☐ LET'S GET INVISIBLE!
- ☐ NIGHT OF THE LIVING DUMMY 2
- ☐ NIGHT OF THE LIVING DUMMY 3
- ☐ THE ABOMINABLE SNOWMAN OF PASADENA
- ☐ THE BLOB THAT ATE EVERYONE
- ☐ THE GHOST NEXT DOOR
- ☐ THE HAUNTED CAR
- ☐ ATTACK OF THE GRAVEYARD GHOULS
- ☐ PLEASE DON'T FEED THE VAMPIRE!
- ☐ THE HEADLESS GHOST
- ☐ THE HAUNTED MASK 2
- ☐ BRIDE OF THE LIVING DUMMY
- ☐ ATTACK OF THE JACK-O'-LANTERNS

SCHOLASTIC.COM/GOOSEBUMPS

Goosebumps

Read them all—if you dare!